I0728357

ISBN: 978-1-944866-06-8

Edited by Christoph Paul & Grant Wamack
Cover Art by Matthew Revert
Interior Design by Joel Amat Güell

THIS BOOK AIN'T NUTTIN TO FUCK WITH: A WU-TANG TRIBUTE ANTHOLOGY

edited by
Christoph Paul and Grant Wamack

INDEX

1

Gabino Iglesias

BIG GHETTO BOYS

When bad men get together to do bad things, the air around them gets thick and smells like the possibility of blood. Every breath is pregnant with the stench of sangre and you can feel it in the back of your throat. The patio I'm sitting in is big and open, the sky over us full of stars long dead, but the air around me smells like la huesuda is aching to make an appearance.

It looks like a party, but it's not.

Half of the folks here are black and don't speak enough Spanish to feel comfortable outside of a taco truck menu. The other half is brown, crossed the border less than 24 hours ago, and have the English skills of a drunk toddler with a speech impediment.

Me? I'm stuck in the middle, playing translator to a bunch of dudes with guns. I look the part, but I was doing day labor until a couple of months ago. Now I'm surrounded by wolves. Los negros are so high on weed they have to look down to see airplanes and some of the Mexicans are sweating as meth or blow runs like a caballo loco through their veins.

Everything about this points to the kind of ending that shows up in the news the next morning. I just want to get the deal closed, collect my roll, and get the fuck outta here.

There's a pretty chola sitting across from me, about ten feet away. Her ass barely fits in the plastic chair she's occupying. She's mouthing the words to the song coming from the two giant speakers set on either side of the sliding door that leads from the house's kitchen to the patio. It's Wu Tang. I watch her red lips move. They drive the words coming from the speakers into my brain.

Small change, they putting shame in the game I take aim and blow that nigga out the frame...

None of the black dudes look at her. They're too busy sharing joints and sipping drinks. The fuckers are wearing hoodies in the middle of the summer in Texas. Dudes who do that are either really stupid, locos, or as dangerous as they come. These guys carry themselves with the swagger of those used to taking lives and not paying for it.

Two of them look like they either played football in college or pushed a lot of iron around in the yard of la casa grande. The tinta on their necks and their current whereabouts tell me it's the second option. They are standing together. Six of them.

They look like they belong in the cover of a hip-hop album, not in this patio in the outskirts of Houston.

They had Wu-Tang blasting when we pulled up to the house, all hard beats, smoking, money, drugs, and gats. Half an hour later, the mix is still going. It blends so well with the rugged atmosphere that the music seems to be naturally emanating from the ground. It makes me nervous. Music that loud is always meant to cover other sounds. The weight of the gun against my hip keeps the paranoia at bay, but the damn thing is still there, buzzing at the edge of my brain like a thousand angry bees.

I keep looking at the chola. She's moving her right hand as she sings along. It looks like she's actually spitting those lines: Method Man with mad cleavage and piernas gordas. I like what I'm seeing. Her thick legs look like they're about to rip her jeans apart and bust out. There's a man's name tattooed on her neck in cursive. Roberto or Rodrigo. Can't tell from here, but it doesn't matter because she's alone. She's been alone since we got here. Maybe she's with one of these black dudes, but I'm pretty sure every woman here is getting paid for their presence. These are all bought smiles and cleavages here to keep the raza dudes mellow. Los vatos que cruzan la frontera to conduct cartel business are friends with death and everyone on this side of the border knows that and tries to keep them happy.

My blood abandons my brain heading down to my crotch making my eyes linger a second too long. Then the chola looks at me. She smiles. Her eyebrows are perfect. All white girls should have a chola friend so they can learn how to do eye and eyebrow makeup. I look away, sink down a bit lower on my chair, and pull out a cigarette. I need to stay sharp. Giving in to the alien bruja magic of the chola's eyes is a sure way of doing exactly the opposite of that. Instead I put a cancer stick in my mouth and fish in my pockets for my lighter as the bass from the speakers starts to match my pulse.

The song ends. I hear a dog bark in the distance and realize no one is talking. The Mexicans that drove up are on edge. Son del cartel de Sinaloa. Bad men. They control most of the drug trade in this part of Texas. There's a huge pickup sitting outside. It holds fifty pounds of meth in tightly wrapped brown packages. Esa mierda se queda aquí. In exchange, they're taking $130,000 and a different pickup back across that dusty chunk of Swiss cheese known as la frontera. With the hundreds pounds of ice sitting at the curb and the chingos de lana somewhere in the house or in a car nearby, I know every pinche cabrón is on edge, waiting for a strange look or a wrong word to be said so they can start shooting. As the Tango Blast say, if you ain't blastin', you ain't lastin'.

I look at the group of men that brought us here. Their numbers keep shifting. Six. Eight. Thirteen. That worries me. I exhale smoke and they look like dark ghosts behind a curtain. I feel a hand on my shoulder and jump.

"Easy, cuz," says a skinny man they call Ghost. "Come in the house for a sec. I need to talk to you real quick."

I don't want to go in the house with him. I don't want to leave the four twitchy Mexicans out here. I don't want to be alone in that house with Ghost and whatever or whoever else is in there. However, I know I have to get up and follow Ghost. Disrespecting one of these motherfuckers could make all this tension turn into a massacre.

"Sure thing, man," I say while getting up.

Ghost turns around and walks toward the kitchen door. He's already between the speakers by the time I'm done getting up. It's like the pinche hijo de puta moves without touching the ground. I follow him into the house. As I approach the speakers, the bass hits me in the chest like a sledgehammer and rattles my eardrums.

Face responsibility… Little ghetto boy, playin in the ghetto street.

Fuck.

I look back at the Mexicans. They're huddled around. Their faces tell me they're way past antsy and their guns are screaming to come out spitting lead. The blacks seem relaxed. They've done this shit before. One of them, a short, chubby fucker with a huge afro they call Lucky, pulls on a blunt, tilts his head back, and releases a creamy cloud of smoke into the air—it twists into a screaming face. A second later the smoke dissipates and the face vanishes.

Lucky then looks at me and winks. The colorful necklaces around his neck are the kind I've only seen on Cubans and Puerto Ricans. I wonder what weird, ancient god he prays to, and I send my own prayer to la Virgencita to keep my ass safe and all my sangre inside my body.

"Yo, you coming or what?" asks Ghost.

I look back at him, nod, and start walking again.

We enter the house and he walks across the kitchen and turns left into a small hallway. He opens the first door on the right. I follow him into a small room. There's a blue couch with a huge television set on a black table in front of it. Ghost sits on the couch. I sit on the opposite side. He reaches into his pocket and I feel tempted to reach for my piece. He pulls out a massive blunt and lights it up, inhales, and offers it to me. I take it and do the same. I want to stay sharp, but not partaking would look shady.

"So what's up, Ghost?"

He looks at me. The right side of his mouth creeps up. His mouth opens and an angry gorilla punches my lungs from the inside. Adrenaline jumps on my veins and mis dedos tingle a bit. La hierba. That shit is laced. PCP would be my best guess. PCP and paranoia son una mala mezcla.

"You're a smart dude, Carlos," Ghost says. "I like you. Word on the streets is you keep your nose clean. No one's out to get you because you don't fuck around with other people's money and shit, you know what I'm saying?"

There is really no correct way to reply to that, so I nod and wait for Ghost to continue. El cabrón has a weird mouth and I think I can see two dark tongues in there instead of one.

"Man, crackers are turning to this Mexican meth you guys keep bringing us because it's cheaper and stronger, you know? This is good business right here. The boys and I are starting our own thing. Fuck the Gangster Disciples, cuz. They stuck on the old ways and the old drugs. They don't wanna pursue all this redneck money. We do. We already have some contacts, but we need someone like you, someone who can be trusted to knock down the language barrier and help us out, help us keep shit nice and clean. We can reach out to smaller cartels and cut down on the price Sinaloa is giving us. Between the half mil we'll make on this batch after cutting and the hundred thou we're keeping from tonight? Shit, son, we're on our way to big business. All I need to know now is if you in, homie…so what's up?"

I don't know exactly what Ghost is asking me to do. The music is coming into the house and filling the space around us. It's a slower, almost mellow beat. It takes me a second to recognize the song. Wu Tang sometimes slows it down to drop heavy shit.

Yo, somethin' in the street went, bang bang …

It sounds like they're sending me a message. It also sounds like Ghost is offering me a job. The sofa feels like it's melting underneath me. The PCP is feeding on my fear.

"So…you offering me a gig or what, man?"

"Fuck yeah, man. It starts now. You get those guys in this room and play it cool. We'll take care of everything. We have enough firepower to put a small cartel to sleep tonight, and there's only four of them. The second they get their asses in here, we put them away. Quick. We keep the ice and the money. You get thirty Gs for your trouble. You contact your amigos in Sinaloa tonight and tell them the deal is done, play it cool. Or don't. Maybe these fuckers out here are supposed to make that phone call. That'd be even better. If they don't call, they might think they're hiding something. I don't give a shit, man. The point is we also tell 'em shit went down, tell them the ice is real good and we want to make business again. We back you up on that, cuz. These four mufuckas took our money and stayed in the country. Ain't that shit the beaner dream anyway? We all clean, and they start looking for those who kept their money. Easy. After this, you ride with us, you make it easy for us to contact the smaller cartels and take over the ice trade in Texas."

Ghost's plan has more holes than la frontera. Sinaloa will smell my bullshit ten miles away. We will all end up in a dirty room in an abandoned house with flies taking a shit on our eyeballs. But If I say that, Ghost and those gorillas outside will do what they want except they'll keep the lana and I'll get a bala between the eyes. I feel something on my eyeballs and know it's the stuff I just smoked. Ese no es buen negocio. I nod slowly. If I say yes, maybe I walk outta here with thirty Gs. That's enough to become invisible for a while, somewhere north of here. If I say no, I'm just pushing my expiration day forward.

"Yeah, man. I'm in. Thirty Gs? Shit, ese, that's more money than I've ever had. Sinaloa isn't stupid, man. You gotta be careful what you say. And I'm making myself scarce for a while."

Ghost looks at me. His eyes probing into mine. I know he wants more. He wants a promise of loyalty because those things are the only currency that matters when you're not talking money. I lift my shirt, pull my piece out slowly, and hold it up. Ghost doesn't move.

"I'll blast with you tonight, homie. I'm fucking in."

I don't want to kill anyone, but I want to walk outta here with the same amount of blood I had when I got here.

Ghost smiles. Hard. His mouth cracks open. He definitely has two tongues. They're either deep blue or purple. I can't tell, but I see two things moving around in his mouth. "Yeah, cuz," he says, "We're gonna treat you right. You open those doors for us, we'll line your pockets."

He doesn't wait for me to reply. Instead, he reaches for the joint and takes a long pull.

"Let's get out there and get this done. Just tell them the money's here and we're ready to do this. Then hang back. Stay by the door once we get back in here."

Ghost stands up and walks to the door. I follow him. The flesh and bone in my legs has been replaced by rubber. I think about the rosary around my neck and the gun in my pants. Both feel useless. We leave the room and walk out onto the patio.

Someone in the back went, clack clack…

I move toward the Mexicans. Their leader looks at me. His name is Mario, but everyone calls him Topo.

"Los negros dicen que están listos, Topo."

There's fire in his eyes. Drops of sweat cover his upper lip. His arms are covered in jailhouse tinta and mensajes about putas, dinero, and amor de madre. He looks like he can take a bullet and still smile at you.

"Afila el ojo, hijueputa. Aquí huele feo. Estos pinches cabrones se traen algo entre manos."

He doesn't have an idea of how right he is, but I'm not about to tell him or feed his paranoia. I shake my head. I know I'll shoot, but I won't aim for him. His ghost is something I don't wanna deal with in this life or the next.

"No, ya me enseñaron la lana," I tell him, letting him know I've seen the money.

Topo smiles. I tell him we're going to pick it up, shake hands, and get the hell outta here in a car they have waiting for us outside. Topo nods, his eyes digging into mine, looking for la verdad and finding I don't know what.

I hear a whistle under the racket and turn to see Ghost by the door. Lucky and the other gorillas are disappearing through the door. I move to follow and Topo grabs my arm.

"A la primera señal de problemas, saca el hierro y dispara."

I nod again. I try to swallow. My throat refuses. I feel a drop of sweat run down my left side, from my armpit to my waist. I know it's a snake.

Topo walks beside me and then I let him enter the house first. Lucky is waiting at the entrance to the hallway. He's smiling. The PCP makes his smile turn into something large and liquid-like that splashes around on his face. Another Mexican pushes past me and stands very close to Topo's back. His hands are moving near his waist like raccoons circling a garbage can.

I hear Ghost say "Entra, amigos! Entra!"

Then Lucky pulls me back by the arm and walks in front of me. The click clack of a gun comes from the track that's playing outside and fries my last nerve. I reach the door in time to see the gorilla in front of Lucky reach into the dark depths of his hoodie and pull out an Uzi. The next ten seconds go by in the blink of an eye. The Uzi spits.

Two heads spit clouds of red gore into the air. The wall beside the door explodes, sending chunks of gypsum board and white dust into the air splattered with blood and brains. Someone screams. I see a brown shaved head turn. I pull my piece, raise it above the mayhem in front of me, and squeeze off a couple of shots. I fucking shoot at the men I'm supposed to be working for, the men who were supposed to pay me at the end of the night, the men who have ties to Sinaloa. It's so fucked up I scream and keep pulling the trigger because violence is the only answer when everything is fucked and nothing makes sense.

I see Topo through the smoke and flashes. Then two shots from something heavier than the Uzi and heavier than my hierro ring out, but those sounds are swallowed as something fully automatic erupts.

The shaved head flies back and disappears, and I realize I'm pressing myself against the wall.

My gun clicks empty and then Lucky smacks me in the back. He's laughing.

Ghost materializes on my right, like he is almost behind me, but I'm not sure if he really is and I jump. He was supposed to be in that room. He hasn't even walked by me this whole time. But he is here and smiles at me and runs two purple tongues across his lips. He hands me a brown paper bag. La lana. I reach out and grab it with shaking hands, my empty gun still in my right hand.

For the first time since we got here, I can't hear the music. I take half a step back and look at the door leading to the patio. The beautiful chola is on the ground, her gorgeous eyes open and unblinking, a brutal gash across her neck. The puddle of blood isn't big because the ground is soaking it up. I see a pair of legs behind the chola. They end in black high heels.

Ghost is saying something about calling me. That someone will take me home. He asks if I want them to take care of the piece and then he pulls it from my hand before I can reply. He tells me someone is waiting outside. That the bodies are going to be wrapped up and hidden in the walls. That the guns will vanish. That I don't have to worry about anything. He smiles again, places a hand on my shoulder, and pushes me toward the door. I think about turning back, but I don't want to see the bodies.

The PCP is kicking against my ribs like an angry mule. Todo se mueve like when you're on a boat.

I manage to get outside and one of the gorillas is waiting for me in a black SUV. I walk to it and get in. My heart has left my throat and inches its way back to my chest. We pull off the curb. The gorilla drives to the end of the streets and asks me where we're going. I point right as I look out the window.

There's a skeletal woman standing on the corner. She looks at me. She has the dead chola's eyes. La huesuda. Her eyes will haunt me. They will follow me forever. I didn't kill the pretty chola, but her death somehow hangs over me. Her brutalized beauty that is no more will follow me. I look for her in la huesuda, but the rest of her face is bones underneath paper-thin white skin. I squeeze the lana tighter against my chest and close my eyes. The horrible thing that just happened is only the beginning and I know it. The gorilla presses a button on the radio. Nothing happens for two seconds. Then the chorus croons from the SUV's speakers.
"Can it be that it was all just so simple."

2

Charles Austin Muir

THE RAEKWONOMICON

"Every hero's tale deserves a prologue."
— The Raekwonomicon

He comes from the League of SorceRZAs in the 36th dimension. The sorceRZAs are masters of mystical chessboxing. They fight The Hidden — the things under reality's stairs created by the Shadow Mastaz, the Shaolin's most powerful magicians.

War is the equalizer, the Dao of the Wu-niverse.

Today's battlefield is Earth. The sorceRZA makes the drop like an occult paratrooper. He starts as vapor, then grows flesh when he touches down. His mission is to track Shaolin movement in The Crawl, an urban hell where the dead lie unburied and the living skulk in the ruins of corrupt politics and economic stagnation. The Crawl is essentially an above-ground cemetery with accommodations for criminals, lunatics and fugitives.

His last defense is his "double," a self-replicating unit on the astral plane that individuates through metabolic growth if needed.

In a few hours, it will be needed.

Things are about to get messy for Ol' Dirty Wan.

"A sorceRZA sees the enemy within."
— The Raekwonomicon

In true form, the sorceRZA out-danced opponents like a 36th-dimension Ali. But in the mundane ring he had two left feet, his human orb's limbic system slows down to process the uncanny.

So though his meta-gut screamed *Danger, Will Robinson*, he gawked at the kid whose moans had drawn him from shelter after dusk. The gangly teenager was scrambling up a telephone pole with ninja speed. Six feet up, Ninja Boy froze, monkey-hugging the moonlit pole.

Something moved under his grass-stained Carmelo Anthony jersey. Ol' Dirty Wan's instincts prayed a desperate *I'm Audi*, but his orb stayed frozen.

The A and Y of the jersey bulged out like vanilla popsicles. Under the popsicles an Alien-burst ruptured through his back in a V formation of long, chitinous stalks that ended in disco ball-sized globes. The kid looked like a junkie mutant cherub wrapped around the telephone pole, one wing high above Ol' Dirty Wan's face.

In human form Ol' Dirty Wan called himself Chuck Morgan.

Morgan's heart skipped a beat when the globes burped ash.

They snowed down on him, and he saw they were more like tiny white petals. Finally Ol' Dirty Wan found the right neuron circuit and sent Morgan back into the building he had come from. He closed his eyes and meditated on his third eye. From his internal viewing room — which resembled a parlor with a mantel bearing his aura shield — he examined his circulatory system and found an unwanted guest.

He went to the shield and drew a cloaking sigil to deflect Shaolin mind readers.

Then he mentally hailed the intruder.

"Stronger than the fist is the power to conversate."
— The Raekwonomicon

I see you. Explain yourself.

EAT A DICK.

You have something to do with the boy on the telephone pole?

EEYUUHHHUHHHUHHHUHHH

Cooperate or I'll raise my healing vibration.

HA, THAT STUFF'S FOR SUCKERS.

Not so.

OWWWW!!! OKAY, RESPECT FOR THE REIKI FINGAZ. WHAT YOU WANT?

What are you?

I'M A PARASITICAL FUNGUS. I PRODUCE A SPORE THAT MANIPULATES THE HUMAN BRAIN. WHEN PEOPLE INGEST ME THEY TURN INTO ZOMBIE SLAVES AND SPREAD ME

AROUND LIKE NOROVIRUS. I'M LIKE JANET JACKSON, MAKIN' MY OWN ZOMBIE RHYTHM NATION.

Why?

SAME REASON FUNGI LIKE ME PREY ON ANT COLONIES HERE ON EARTH. IT'S THE DAO. CH-CHICK-POW!

Who's behind this?

NAH, I AIN'T GOIN' THERE…

Who?

OWWWWWW!!! ENOUGH WITH THE WOO WOO SQUEEZE! YOUR BROTHER, AIIGHT? MYND RECKA.

You speak the truth. You may go.

OH THANK YOU BOSS, THANK YOU. I'M A DEPART NOW. BUT YOU AND ME, WE AIN'T DONE. IN 24 HOURS I'M BRINGIN' SOME HARD, PIPE HITTIN', BRAIN CELL EATIN' NIGGAS. THE DEATH DREAM ANGEL IS GETTING MEDIEVAL ON YOUR —

Ol' Dirty Wan closed his mental viewing room, preserving the sigil on his aura shield.

He looked down at the junkie mutant cherub clenched around the telephone pole beneath the second-story window.

"The road to salvation is fraught with illusion."
— The Raekwonomicon

Ol' Dirty Wan walked into the brownfield on The Crawl's south side. The Stink was three miles of mothballed contamination that used to give wayfarers tumors. The barren landscape reflected his thoughts. He saw only one way to avoid becoming the Death Dream Angel's zombie slave — place his orb in permanent quarantine.

He looked around at the other unwitting victims streaming from The Crawl. The Death Dream Angel was directing them to the surrounding communities. Nothing, not even bodily destruction, could prevent their transformation into biological weapons. His brother, Mynd Recka, was the Shaolin's top pestilence maker. He created infectious diseases and plagues like the military built Humvees.

"You've got a sickness, man," his brother told him in the Battle of Liquid Swords on Neptune. "You're like that hippie sorceRZA from Nazareth — hurting yourself for suckers, bleeding for the sake of bleeding."

If bleeding maintained the cosmic balance, Ol' Dirty Wan would bleed till the end of time.

The time for his orb would come much sooner, though. By sunrise Morgan would resemble Ninja Boy. Already he had a cough, like his fellow travelers, which The Stink, long considered safe for passage, could not account for. He had visions, too, photographically distinct impressions of Vanessa crawling toward him. His old girlfriend was nude and filthy, with dead leaves in her hair. Each time she collapsed on the prickly grass before she could reach him. Chitinous stalks burst from her spine.

She looked like an angel who had jumped off her cloud because her wings were useless and revolting. This was Mynd Recka's modus operandi, a looped waking nightmare meant to shake him through his mind's eye.

"Man, you look like you've seen a ghost."

Zombie Vanessa vanished. In her place stood a ruddy, balding man with a dirty bandage around his left thumb. Craggy muscles glistened with sweat under his overalls. "We all have, right? Come on, I know where we can catch a ride. I'll drop you anywhere's south of here."

Ol' Dirty Wan pitied the doomed man, who had a gap in his front teeth.

"That would be great. I'm in a bit of a hurry, actually."

"Our ultimate goal is disarmament."
— The Raekwonomicon

Not all the wanderers were infected. "Mac" turned out to be a parasite himself, a sexual vampire. Together, with two men lying in wait, he attacked Ol' Dirty Wan outside an abandoned factory. The sorceRZA took down the gang-rapists with Tiger Style kung fu.

He should have run a mind scan on Mac first, but Vanessa's phantasm had rattled him. He told himself to stay focused while he drove his psychokinetically hot-wired pickup truck out of The Stink. Outside of Tical, the nearest town, he ran out of gas. Walking into town, he sent out psychical feelers.

"That's how you locate the enemy," his brother told him before the Schism. "A warrior stays focused by transferring mental anguish to his double. This causes a cosmic energy shift — a kind of heat signature. You project personally disturbing imagery to the suspected area and read for fluctuations."

Ol' Dirty Wan let the trauma of "seeing" a crawling-dead Vanessa dissolving in his orb. He had taught himself to absorb emotions organically, knowing his brother's tactics.

His own psychical feelers operated in reverse. He showed Tical's residents a world without The Crawl and men like Mac. Where food abounded and citizens greeted each other on the street. Feasts ran for days, wine flowed, stories were told and the sun rose and set in smog-free plumage. His images worked beneath conscious perception, to avoid valuations that might dim the collective energy he wanted to use.

Associations outside his control faded in. People smiling, animals playing… loving memories of the departed. The townspeople's unconscious affection emitted a golden light, which Ol' Dirty Wan drew into a telepathic sigil upon a B-17 bomber plane mounted on blocks in the town square. The de-weaponized memorial fit his intention behind the sigil.

"Help me find a gravedigger."

"Cash rules everything around me. This is true in all universes."
— The Raekwonomicon

The midday sun blazed down on Tical. Odors of struggle choked the hot streets like the stink of emotional compost bins.

Ol' Dirty Wan's psychical feelers had nourished the townspeople's energy bodies. But the physical ones still sagged under their burdens. His best option was a big kid with meth sores outside a convenience store. He took one glance back at the bomber spreading its dead wings over the cityscape. Then he walked toward the tweaker.

Before he could speak, the ground shook.

BOOOOOOMMM. BOOOOOMMM. Like ghost pilots attacking Tical with its landmark. Ol' Dirty Wan turned the corner toward the source. Down the street, inside a garage, a man lifted a barbell from the floor and returned it. The crash rocked the block. He turned away and clasped his hands behind his shaved head. Tattooed across his broad brown back was the word SARDONICAZ.

Ol' Dirty Wan scanned the man's mind. He saw acute awareness of death and empathy for the sick. And books. The covers were cartoon drawings. They showed headless corpses, men in pig masks and beasts with Brobdingnagian erections. Under the titles was the word in his tattoo.

A writer, he thought. Imaginative.

Morbidly inclined.

Able-bodied.

Play it smart.

"Mr. Sardonicaz?"

"Ha, no. Name's Curtis. How can I help?"

Curtis's smile was an eggshell over his aggression toward the tall shabbily dressed stranger in his driveway. Speaking softly, Ol' Dirty Wan presented himself as eccentric millionaire, Chuck Morgan.

"I'm the founder of Ol' Dirty Fitness. You've heard of it? No? Well, anyway, I have a proposition."

Seated on a bench in Curtis's sweltering garage, he made it.

"Just so I understand," Curtis said. "You want me to bury you in a coffin in The Stink?"

"Nine feet deep," Chuck Morgan said.

"Then leave you?"

"Like I said, I'm an escape artist. It's part of my workout."

"You've got a coffin?"

"Your town must have a mortuary."

"What about transport?"

"A pickup truck. It needs gas, though."

"Don't take this the wrong way, Mr. Morgan, but I have a hard time believing you're a millionaire fitness guru."

Chuck Morgan grabbed the barbell and pulled it to standing. Then he set it down and handed Curtis several C-notes from his jeans pocket.

"You didn't just do that. Lift six-hundred pounds one-handed."

"And I didn't just give you enough C.R.E.A.M. to buy yourself a mode of transport."

"My niece needs it more. She's going through chemo and my loser-ass brother won't help with medical costs. Fine, you've got a gravedigger." Curtis extended his hand. "Funny. I write books under a pen name. Sardonicaz, like my tattoo says. It's inspired by a fictional character who goes insane after he digs up his father's corpse."

"Meditation exists to help Ol' Dirty (M.E.T.H.O.D.)."
— The Raekwonomicon

Chuck Morgan waited in the driveway while Curtis biked to the highway with a gas can. Curtis returned with the pickup and stowed the bike in the garage. They bought a casket at the town mortuary. Morgan paid extra to avoid inquiries.

The bribe, like Curtis's C-notes, was an illusion. But so was all money. C.R.E.A.M. existed because people agreed to believe in it. Ol' Dirty Wan was protecting them from an apocalyptic infection by manipulating the fantasy. That was how he rationalized deceiving men like Curtis. If he came out of this, he would tell Curtis his powers, which reached even into cyberspace. Curtis would be devastated, but he would know the truth. His paranoid energy would reflect reality rather than the conundrum of a stranger who frightened him.

Morgan bought supplies at a hardware store. Then they drove into The Stink.

They parked near the abandoned factory. Mac and his accomplices were gone. Curtis sat on the tailgate and chomped on a sub.

"I'm gonna lay this on the table and then shut

up," he said. "First, my dream: you're the real deal. I couldn't find anything about you on the Internet, but that doesn't mean you aren't about to do something amazing. A strongman escape artist built like Jimmie Walker? Man, you should have a reality show.

"Second, my nightmare: this is your elaborate way of rolling up on me and you've read too much Edgar Allan Poe."

"If it makes you feel better," Chuck said, "meet me at the bomber at dawn. I'll tell you how I did it."

He'd meant to arrange the meeting with sigil magic, but Curtis's nerves were on edge.

While Curtis toiled with pick and shovel, Ol' Dirty Wan meditated. He returned to his third eye's viewing room. Next to the cloaking sigil on his aura shield he drew a cutting sigil to break his brother's connection with the fungus. He couldn't afford to let the two link since the Death Dream Angel had reached his brain.

When he woke from his trance, the sun had dipped behind the wall surrounding the new industrial complex to the west. A lone guard tower stood against the Martian-red sky. War was in the air. It called to Ol' Dirty Wan through the smog, The Stink's rotten-egg stench, the steel-meets-dirt noise of Curtis's labors.

Could he avoid a mystical showdown with Mynd Recka?

His brother's psychical feelers took on the quality of a Japanese horror movie. Several times Vanessa's undead ringer climbed from the deepening grave and crawled toward him. In sunset's Grand Guignol hues, she perished in muted agony. Fungus wings Alien-burst from her back and rained spores upon the poisoned earth.

When Curtis had dug the hole to nine feet, Ol' Dirty Wan threw a rope down. He looked into the pit and wondered if he had the strength to transcend what it symbolized. Mynd Recka's Vanessa loop had exhausted him, and his orb's immune system had started a fever to fight infection. His powers were low. Still, he managed to move the rope psychokinetically while pretending to pull on it. Curtis climbed from the hole. His expression turned from admiration to dismay.

"The Stink doesn't seem good for you," he said.

Morgan started to reassure him, then burst out coughing.

They dropped the casket into the hole by moonlight. Morgan climbed down the rope, lifted the lid and stood inside. He stripped off his clothes, except for his briefs, and tossed them up to Curtis who laid them nearby.

"They get in the way," he said.

"You sure you want to go through with this?"

"I'm sure. But first tell me this: who is Jimmie Walker?"

"Sometimes one must bring the ruckus."
— The Raekwonomicon

Spiritually as well as physically, Ol' Dirty Wan was tired. His eons-long life had been spent battling the Shaolin. The darkness and sound of dirt hitting the casket soothed him. He wondered how it would feel to be eternally at peace, free from emotions he refused to shift onto his double or convert to martial energy like his brother.

But practice taught him to shut down his inner martyr. The willingness to self-sacrifice, that in its positive manifestation drove him to do the League's dirty work. Hence the name — Ol' Dirty Wan, who chased The Hidden through the slaughterhouses and sewers of reality to maintain the cosmic balance. He volunteered for the League's grimiest missions, often lethal assignments for his orbs.

Despite his meta-level control, his body panicked. He calmed it with deep breaths and focused on his brow chakra. He called on light from Bobby Digital, his favorite star, to beam into an opening in the crown of his head. Then he created grounding cords, intangible energy tubes running from the base of his spine and major organs into the earth. Heaven and earth qi would stabilize him while the orb bore the physical brunt of mystical pugilism.

He opened his internal viewing room. The sigils on his aura shield were gone. In the back of the room was a door. It did not belong here. He turned the knob. He entered an apartment, his old place with Vanessa. Her books were stacked neatly on the nightstand and her clothes littered the floor. Frankincense burned on the dresser. On their wall bed a beefy blonde man was sodomizing her so hard the hinges rattled. He had paintball-red eyes and gold teeth.

"What up, bitch." The voice was the Death Dream Angel's.

He jerked Vanessa's head back. Her mascara ran from crying. She broke free and jumped out the window.

Screams rang out four stories below.

Ol' Dirty Wan pointed at the grinning rapist. "You're not even a ghost."

The scene vanished in black smoke.

White light flickered. Now he was strapped to a chair in a room with stainless steel walls. A soiled mattress lay by the door. The overhead bulb faltered. By its weak light he read the upside-down words on the straitjacket binding him under his restraints: PROPERTY OF THE SHADOW MASTAZ. The door opened, and Vanessa crawled onto the mattress, nude and covered in semen. Her face was a sleepwalker's. The Death Dream Angel strode in after her, his limp penis dangling between his knees. Then Ol' Dirty Wan's near-spitting image entered, wearing a black trench coat.

"Nice cloaking job," Mynd Recka said. "It took me three counter-sigils to find you."

His partner threw up the Shaolin's S sign. "Told you I'd be back, dawg. I work faster when you irritate me."

Faintly, like distant thunder, Ol' Dirty Wan felt the vibrations of earth piling on his casket.

He said, "Let's do this."

Mynd Recka shed the trench coat. His prick stiffened to elephantine dimensions. "I've developed a new technique," he said.

"The Vlad Style." The Death Dream Angel stroked himself.

The pair resembled the monsters in Curtis's books.

Mynd Recka moved sullenly to the mattress. He was conserving energy. He had made a bold move preempting their mystical chessboxing ring. Ol' Dirty Wan recalled the Battle of the Cuban Linx Moon where his brother had exhausted all his power on illusions. His ego always betrayed him, like the heat signatures he studied. Still, he had turned Vanessa's memory into a potent thought form.

The Death Dream Angel launched into villain-monologue.

"So here we are in the Mystical Matrix. Only this artificial reality is twice as strong with my bacterial kung fu. I'm all up in your brain now, Neo, swimmin' in your psychology. Your problem is you're capable of love. Whereas my man here turns everything to hate. He even hates you because he can't love like you do. I know this because he made me." He butted his fists together. "My old man and my uncle, two of the best in the business showing the light and dark side of catching feelings. But you know darkness always wins, right?"

"Suck this dick," Mynd Recka said to Vanessa.

The Death Dream Angel made an absurd sight expounding on darkness with a monstrous boner.

"Darkness don't get hurt. It don't fall in love while it's posing undercover as a student. It don't get shocked neither when it walks in on the bitch with some old fat fuck who's grading her on a different curve than the rest of the class reading David Foster Wallace."

"Kurt Vonnegut," Ol' Dirty Wan said.

"My bad. Wrong memory bank." The Death Dream Angel moved behind Vanessa, who snaked half his cock down her throat. "Anyway, darkness don't cry neither when the slut jumps off a bridge three days later. But that's okay, we're gonna make this right." He winked his paintball eye at Ol' Dirty Wan and flashed gold teeth. "We're gonna show your girl how darkness romances."

Ol' Dirty Wan tested the straitjacket. Mynd Recka had charged it with a binding spell. His brother was using humiliation to steal his power. He and his partner mirrored each other slamming Vanessa in ass and mouth. Ol' Dirty Wan was to be the unwilling test audience for a gangbang porno in Third Eyemax.

"Take my big fat novel, girl," the Death Dream Angel said. "Infinite Jizz!"

"No, no, *Slaughter Ass Five*." Mynd Recka winked at Ol' Dirty Wan. "Right, brother?"

He watched them smack, slap and jackhammer Vanessa at both ends. A vile caricature of the unfaithful act he had caught the real woman at. "My psychic projections," his brother once boasted, "are nothing to fuck with." The tactic worked despite his cognizance. Victim energy buzzed under Ol' Dirty Wan's straitjacket like a bee swarm. Guilt, betrayal and other deeply buried emotions stung him.

He should not have fallen in love. He should not have shown weakness. He should not have mocked Vanessa when she begged forgiveness. He should not have left her alone the night she killed herself. He should not have argued when the League found his cloaking sigil and extracted him.

"Oh shit, Neo," the Death Dream Angel shouted. "I'm about to bust! *Ch-chick-pow!*"

He should not —

"Witness the strength, brother. Vlad Style, impaling your psyche."

— *let Mynd Recka win.*

"I forgive you, Vanessa," he said. "If you'll forgive me. Help me." Ol' Dirty Wan's tearful invocation broke the chair straps.

He stood.

"Help me forgive myself for my imperfections. Help me release the pain that binds us. Help me give it all to my brother… with the Franken Style."

His sleeves expanded like balloons. They snapped apart. Gulliver-sized hands shot through the openings. The straitjacket split down the middle, rendered by his swelling bulk. Rivets poked from the crown of his head, and his grin made a wound of jagged yellow teeth.

The sperm-soaked automaton with Vanessa's face vanished. Gulliver hands extended, Ol' Franken Dirty advanced on Mynd Recka and the Death Dream Angel. Their flesh opened to the monster like ripe peaches.

Darkness again.

Victory slammed Ol' Dirty Wan back into his dying body. Terminal fever screamed in his nerve cells. His joints throbbed, his hands shook and his teeth chattered a beat that rang to the roof of his skull. He had died many deaths and each one felt horrible. He slowed his breaths to conserve oxygen. His muscles strained. The fungus gave him steroid-strength to break free but his grounding cords held firm. His brother had failed to sever them while he tormented Ol' Dirty Wan in illusion.

Heaven and earth qi flushed enemy poison out through his grounding cords.

Ol' Dirty Wan clapped his hands to his temples. Bobby Digital light burned the zombie toxins in his brain.

GODDAMN REIKI FINGAZ, the Death Dream Angel cursed in his mind. Then he said to his brother: "I forgive you, too," and the last he heard was Mynd Recka mutter, "just like that hippie sorceRZA from Nazareth," before his consciousness left his body.

The orb expired. Stalks burst through its chest and punched through the casket lid. Ol' Dirty Wan's spirit beat them to the surface and jumped into his astral double by the mound. He watched as the ground shuddered.

The fungus bomb exploded harmlessly, beneath the surface.

"Thank you," he said, to no one and everyone.

"If the odds are in your favor, you're fighting the wrong fight."
— The Raekwonomicon

Ol' Dirty Wan climbed onto the wing of the bomber and sat beside Curtis. They watched the sun rise. Morning traffic thickened and shopkeepers opened their doors. A cloaking sigil rendered the two men invisible. Ol' Dirty Wan explained everything — from his insertion in The Crawl to his triumph over Mynd Recka. "The value of nine has a power over my brother similar to the Poetic Wave Principle, but don't ask me to explain it."

Curtis buried his head in his hands when the sorceRZA finished his account.

"I always wanted to write something like this, but you're telling me it's real. Some Michael Moorcock parallel universe shit."

"The fungus turns people into infectious spore

bombs. The only way we can stop it is to safely detonate each one."

"By burying them."

"Nine feet deep."

"But it's spread into the cities."

"A lot of digging to be done."

Curtis stood and propped a foot on the plane's port inner engine. "You barely kept your old body from breaking to the surface. How's this going to work with normal people?"

"You dig, I chessbox."

"Sardonicaz and Ol' Dirty Wan," Curtis said. "We sound like a rap group."

Ol' Dirty Wan flashed his new orb's gold front tooth. "The dirtiest."

3

Joshua Chaplinsky

SUPREME MATHEMATICS: A CIPHER

A girl with a sword walks through the forest at night. Her thoughts hum like bees in a hive.

Part 1: Knowledge

Sifu taught me that Knowledge, represented by the number one, is the accumulation of facts through experience and observation. Empirical data reinforces the foundation of all existence, for matter must be "known" in order for it to manifest. "A *tudi* must know the ledge," *Sifu* told me during my *Bai Shi* ceremony, "with such a high degree of certainty that even if the ground gave way, they would avoid falling into the abyss of ignorance."

The number one also represents Man. *Sifu* believed that Man is the Sun at the center of our solar system. From what I have observed in my own experience, I do not hold this to be true. Because if Man is the Sun, we are presented with a paradox, simultaneously supporting both the heliocentric and anthropocentric scientific models. The next thing you know people will be insisting the Earth is flat again.

I raised these and other concerns a number of times, but a lowly *tudi* must know their place as well as the ledge. I grew to resent my station, and ultimately decided to express my dissatisfaction with the sword. As I worked my *jian* up inside him, separating his heart into two halves, I could see the uncertainty in his face. I then put my hands inside his chest and rent the two halves into four, separating atria and ventricles into distinct chambers, which I arranged like a puzzle next to his body. The light faded from his eyes and the abyss swallowed him whole. My true training had begun.

She rests her weight on the jian like a staff, the blunt wooden edges of the practice blade stained a dark red. It leaves a small divot in the dirt with each step. Anyone following her trail would think they tracked an invalid, or an old man with a cane. She would have the element of surprise over any pursuers that underestimated her.

Part 2: Wisdom

Sifu taught me that Wisdom is Knowledge acted upon, which is why I ended his life. I took action based on my Knowledge of his failings as a teacher and human being, on his refusal to release me from my obligation as a *tudi*.

Wisdom is also Water, the vital building block of

life that flows over and around all obstacles. Wisdom is represented by the number two, which also represents Woman.

Sifu believed that Wisdom was the Moon to Knowledge's Sun, a secondary source of light for the misguided people of the world. But the Moon does not need the Sun's light to exist. She carries out her plans in the dark. In darkness I explored the four chambers of my own heart, groping blindly through the mass of throbbing gristle on my path to enlightenment.

The moon peeks through the tree canopy to light the girl's way, but her feet already know the path. She closes her eyes and lets her instincts take over. She wields her jian like a blind man's cane, feeling for any object that might obstruct her path. Her nimble feet tread just as silent without sight.

Part 3: Understanding

Sifu taught me that complete comprehension comes from the addition of Knowledge and Wisdom (1+2=3). The number three also represents the natural byproduct of Man and Woman's union: a Child. As I would come to learn, many purposefully misinterpreted this equation.

Before I put my sword through *Sifu*'s heart, I listened to the heartbeat of our unborn child. I closed my eyes, wandering its four undeveloped compartments. Even at six weeks old, it possessed such strength.

Sifu also taught me that the highest form of Understanding is Love. This much we agreed upon. Love helped me Understand what I needed to do. But his claim that the foundation of Understanding is Knowledge (i.e.: Man) was a misguided lie. Because he could never Know or Understand the pain he put me through.

The bundle slung across her back coos in her ear. She looks over her shoulder at the child and smiles. "It won't be long now," she tells it. "Just a little further and we can rest." The child emits a happy gurgle in response to its mother's voice.

Part 4: Freedom

Sifu taught me that the number four represents Freedom. According to him, Understanding stems from Knowledge, and when you combine the two you get Freedom (1+3=4). But more than one path to Freedom exists, and I did not approve of an equation that included Man and Child but not Woman. I prefer (2-1)+3=4. Wisdom minus Knowledge plus Understanding. A beating heart with its own four chambers. An expanse with enough room for only me and my Child.

The girl loosens the straps of the mei tai and swings the bundle around to her front. The hungry child reaches for her breast before she can even pull up her shirt. As the child feeds, the girl chews on a piece of dry meat and looks out across the forest. The sound of the wind through the leaves overtakes the buzzing in her head and she experiences a moment of calm.

Part 5: Power/Refinement

Power is a force of creative energy. To Refine is to

perfect. The number five, or Power, also represents Truth. Wisdom and Understanding give you Power (2+3=5).

I interpret this as Mother and Child equals Power. A more perfect force than the creation of a Child does not exist, and that is the Truth. When I feel my child's fully formed heart beating against mine, all is right with the world. It bears a resemblance to the developing muscle I explored during my pregnancy, but these four chambers require their own navigation to Understand.

After the child finishes feeding, they continue on their way. The girl sings to the child, softly, so as not to give away their position. Within moments the content child falls asleep. Every snapping branch draws the girl's attention, but she remains calm, her mind in tune with the forest. Every sound has a source, and she can recognize when one does not belong.

Part 6: Equality

Equality is the state of being Equal or possessing Equilibrium. *Sifu* taught that we must strive to reach Equality with all of existence. We achieve this through Knowledge, Wisdom and Understanding, signified by the equation (1+2=3)+(1+2=3)=6.

In an ideal world every Man, Woman, and Child would live in harmony with every other Man, Woman, and Child, but the math is inherently flawed if one and two are not equal from the outset. With the Moon relegated to secondary status, Equilibrium does not exist. We must consider the heart of the other, an additional four chambers that must be passed through, each with their own lesson to impart.

Six can also represent The Devil, as He has the power to be Equal to Man, but not to God. Man may strive for Equality, but a bit of The Devil resides in every man, which undermines his righteousness. Although he hid it well, *Sifu* had more than a bit of The Devil in him.

The girl stops short as she recognizes a sound that does not belong to the forest—a human voice, carried on the wind. Her muscles tense. Where there is one voice there are usually two or more. The child senses her apprehension, shifts in its sleep, but doesn't wake. The girl continues forward at a slower pace, straining her ears to hear as her thoughts prepare to swarm. She regulates her breathing to calm them.

Part 7: God/Perfection

If The Devil is six, then God is seven. God is Perfection, the Supreme Being that created our universe, an assertion art and nature upholds. A few examples: G is the seventh letter of the alphabet. God sees with the seven colors of the rainbow. He hears with the seven notes of the musical scale. Love plus Freedom equals God (3+4=7).

But for some, God represents the opposite of Freedom. I would argue that God could also be considered Equal to Man, as a bit of God exists in every Man, demanding to be worshipped. That, of course, would mean God is also Equal to the Devil, an idea many are not willing to entertain.

I think *Sifu* would have agreed with this. I believe God and The Devil waged a constant battle inside him.

It makes me wonder about myself. Am I my own God, because I dare to choose my own path?

In the end, it has four chambers like everyone else's, but who can Know the heart of God? All students endure this struggle, as they must answer to the God inside the Teacher, and the Teacher's God as well, all while serving the God within themselves.

The girl crouches at the edge of the clearing. A flicker of light illuminates the abandoned temple. A fire. Two men warm themselves beside it with their backs to her. She watches them for some time. Are these the type of men with a bit of God in them, or The Devil? She checks the straps on her mei tai and tightens her grip on her jian.

Part 8: Build/Destroy

To Build is to elevate the mentality and material of one's self and others. By doing so, we can vicariously elevate the planet. To Destroy is to ruin the same by allowing negativity to outweigh the positive. By exercising our Freedom, *Sifu* taught, we can either Build or Destroy (4+4=8). Self Destruction and Destruction of others are often considered one and the same.

But *Sifu* failed to explain that sometimes you need to tear down the old before you can Build something new. So I Destroyed our relationship to facilitate a better life for our Child. For a time our two hearts beat as one, the eight chambers existing as four. But after a thorough examination I decided to destroy those chambers to protect my Child, preventing a further reduction of twelve to four.

The girl sneaks up on the unsuspecting men, jian at the ready. The crackle of the fire masks the sound of her footfall. Before he realizes what is happening, blows to pressure points on the head and neck paralyze the first man. The second flees the scene, limping. The girl holds the wooden sword to the first man's throat. After her long journey, she does not have the strength it would take to run him through, but he doesn't know that. In fact, he might not even be aware the sword is a practice blade. The girl fixes him with a look that says Never come back and releases his body from its paralysis with another series of blows. He scurries off into the darkness after his companion.

Part 9: Birth

To be Born is to be brought into existence. It takes nine months to produce a Child. No other number gives Birth to itself. $9+9=18(1+8=9)$. $9\text{x}9=81(8+1=9)$.

But if nine gives Birth to itself, does that render Man and Woman superfluous? You can't have a Child without Birth. Can you have Birth without a Child? Does that make the act of conception itself immaculate?

And what of Rebirth? Surely the gestation periods must vary. Because Rebirth requires a change of heart, a heart which must then also be explored. And no two hearts are the same. Due to the uncertainty factor, these final four chambers are the most difficult to traverse, the hardest lessons for a student to absorb.

Rebirth times Freedom. 9 hearts x 4 chambers = 36

The girl resists the urge to rest by the fire. Instead she approaches the gravestone at the back of the property. She slings the mei tai around to her front, the child only just stirring. She holds it out to the stone. "Say hello to your father," she tells the child.

Part 0: Cipher

Sifu taught me one final lesson before his demise: Lesson zero. I consider it the most important lesson of all.

The nought represents a Cipher or code, the completion of a circle consisting of 360 degrees (made up of equal parts Knowledge, Wisdom, and Understanding, 120 degrees each).

Existence flows in a continual circle, a snake devouring its own tail, and all in existence makes up the key to Decipher life's encryption.

In other words, to Know your future is to Know your past. Which brings us right back to where we started: Knowledge.

The child yawns and falls back asleep. The girl turns towards the empty temple. "I am home, Sifu," she says. "My training is complete."

4

Mame Bougouma Diene

BEATS, BONES, AND BRISKET

The crack-whore shivered in the corner of the dim project basement; her glittering, purple dress, stiff with dry vomit. Her pimp's face was stony marble, but his eyes had blurred over, his handcuffs barely rattling against the pipe anymore, over the instrumental of "Shadow Boxing."

Smoke burned their eyes, but it was all they could do not to stare at the two teenagers who'd kidnapped them, stirring a foul smelling cauldron in the middle of the room.

"You gotta boil them more, Jaquelin."

"Are you sure those are Baby Jesus's bones?" Jaquelin responded "I'm saying, Phil, they look a little fresh don't you think? ODB's bones should look like Swiss cheese by now. Government Swiss cheese."

"He was buried with voodoo rites. His bones don't

age, they age back, like he's really baby Jesus, got it?"

"But why we gotta kill a crack-whore and her pimp? Jesus had plenty of hooker friends, the real Jesus and Baby Jesus."

"Bodies are bodies. Boil the bones, and mix them with the 'essence of the street'." Philippe said. "That's what the mambo said. If you ask me, pimp and hooker blood is just that."

"Yeah, but then we gotta drink the broth!"

"Yup, voodoo is some sick shit, but we'll have the power of ODB, and then find the remaining members… and do it all over again…Now, where's my axe…"

They call me Big J mackin'/ The Haitian Gatlin/ The best thing to happen to rappin' since scratchin'/

"Killer set boys, killer set." The club owner told Philippe and Jaquelin, aka DJ Samedi and MC Cimetière "How you manage to spin like that without burning your fingers off is beyond me."

That's because we just had Ghostface Killah for lunch, Philippe thought, winking at Jaquelin, then removing a lingering bit of sinew stuck between his teeth with his tongue, trailing a little bit of fat and flavor. They needed a new meat grinder, and fast.

"It's all love, Boss. Records are meant to be spun, and I do the spinning."

The power was intoxicating, and since barbequing Ghostface and skewering U-God, Philippe wasn't just on a hunt for musical perfection, he was on a hunt. Jaquelin feasted as well, but he didn't feel the same satisfaction. Jaquelin ate what he needed, the flesh around finger bones mostly. He was in it for the skills. Philippe would eat the leftovers, and leave some for later.

The records didn't just spin; they glided. The slightest touch of his hand, and the perfect scratch would bring back ghosts of '79 and bootleg turntables.

But Jaquelin looked eager to go, and dinner would be late.

"Yeah." Jaquelin said "We'll take that money now. You know to hit us up when you need another full set of bangers."

"I'm soaked in degrees of knowledge polished by sun-rays. You can't extinguish the flame."

Philippe shoved a doo-rag into Masta Killa's mouth.

"Li te chita pale twop." He said.

Jaquelin nodded, sharpening a knife.

"You know, Noodles?" he said, addressing Masta Killa, "That's actually my favorite verse of yours. Off Immobilarity, right?" He walked up behind him.

Killa had been easier to catch than Ghostface and U-God. Starky Love was trouble, even sedated the man was like a pit-bull, ready to bite your hand off. Killa had gone down easy, a couple of sedatives in his drink and they were good. But you had to admire his stoicism. Ghost threatened them till his last breath. Universal God Allah had surprised them by blessing them. Killa just watched

Jaquelin reach behind him with his blade and didn't even blink. The man was Zen, no doubt about it. They all had a power alright. In death, the truth—or something like that.

"No, no, no!" Philippe intervened before Jaquelin routinely sliced his throat. "We gotta drain him." He pulled out a small tap, attached to a hollowed out spike. Masta Killa blinked.

"Blood pudding!" Jaquelin said, dropping his knife and throwing his hands up. "Fuck no, man!"

"Gotta do what the Mambo said," he said tossing him the tap, over a trembling Masta Killa. "It's worked pretty good so far."

Jaquelin caught the tap looking about to puke, but the glimmer in his eyes was unmistakable. The best thing to happen to rappin' since scratchin'…right…Philippe thought.

Masta Killa kept his eyes closed, repeating the Supreme Mathematics on a rote: Knowledge, Wisdom, Understanding, Culture…

"One precise stab in the external jugular, and then you turn on the tap. Got it?" Philippe asked.

"Got it." Jaquelin answered, his eyes glazed over.

He lifted the tap, its shadow reflecting on the basement wall across from Masta Killa. The shadow of Jaquelin's arm dropped. Killa started screaming.

Briefly.

Then he gurgled.

"This blood pudding is nas-ty." Jaquelin said, helping himself to a second serving.

"Yeah man, my bad, thought I had the recipe down." Philippe replied, wiping his lips.

"Good thing the next one is steak. We can get a good marinade going, throw some spices in there…"

"I told you storming the studio was a bad idea!" Jaquelin said, shaking his head at the carnage.

Raekwon lay on the floor next to the couch, the bullet in his abdomen leaking fluids through his DKNY shirt. Meth had tried to run for it, tripped and knocked himself out against the mixing console. Inspectah Deck hadn't made it; his brain slid down the window panel facing the live room. Four more bodies lay dead in the control room.

They could deal with Johnny Blaze later, but they had to eat The Chef before he could control them.

"Quick!" Philippe screamed, "Get a bite before he talks, or we're fucked!"

"But we were supposed to steak and marinade him!"

"Oh, you muthafuckaz, you done shot the God…" Raekwon mumbled, his hands slipping off the wet patch of blood on his shirt.

"No time for that! As long as he can talk, he's got all the power. Raekwon means gifted with words, that's why we keep buying his albums even though he makes. No. Sense!"

"Yo my flow mad dope like coco/ I eat mad Rollos/ Drag your bitch by her cornrows/ Space bound ships with afros/ We mad quick…" Kwon spit, freezing Jaquelin and Philippe in their tracks, little spurts of blood gushing from his wound with every word.

"See what I mean?!" Philippe yelled.

"I kinda always thought he was the best in the bunch…" Jaquelin stared absently, before shaking himself. "Fuck! You're RIGHT!"

Philippe's teeth landed in Raekwon's cheek before he could drop another rhyme, ripping through his week old stubble like a lawnmower, and into the chubby flesh beneath it.

Jaquelin then grabbed an ankle, and bit into his calf.

"Boy…dude is foul." Jaquelin said, spitting little bits of body hair.

Philippe didn't answer; some of Raekwon's tongue was poking out the hole in his cheek. He bit into it firmly, thrust his neck, and ripped the bloody organ out.

"Why, you little cannibalizing hood rats, I will fuckin'…" Method Man started, coming slowly to his senses.

Jaquelin knocked him out with the butt of his gun.

Raekwon stopped breathing. Philippe swallowed down the rest of his tongue. "Alright, think we better get out of here now. God bless soundproofing." he said.

"What we gonna do about Rollie Fingers, though?" Jaquelin asked, pointing at Deck's missing brains.

Philippe paused and said, "We'll make due with

Cappadonna. Let's get Meth out of here."

Meth awoke to realize he was hanging from the ceiling in a project basement stained with blood and soot. He instinctively reached for his leg pocket and his cell.

"Trying to call Redman?" Philippe laughed. "Ain't gonna happen."

Blaze's eyes were redder than they'd ever been when he was blazed. Two angry cherries about to pop.

"His eyes are about to blow out." Jaquelin said.

"I know. They look delicious don't they?" Philippe heard himself say.

Meth swung against the hook holding the rope tied to his legs.

"Don't fret, Meth." Jaquelin said. "We'll leave your eyes out of this. It's your brain we're picking, and apparently we need you to watch…" He then turned to Philippe, and asked. "Do we really need him to watch?"

"Yes." Philippe answered, much to his regret.

Meth laughed. It echoed strangely, bouncing off the basement walls, creating a rhyme of its own.

"I bring the pain from the brain. Hardcore as you well know. You little niggas, and I DON'T use the word lightly, can choke on it."

He attempted to spit a gob of blood and mucus, but hanging upside down, gravity asserted itself, and it hit his nose, dripping from his face, to his forehead, to the ground.

Philippe shook his head and hit play on the stereo.

Watch these rap niggas…

Meth laughed some more.

"Brain sorbet?" Meth laughed again. "You muthafuckaz dumb eighties, yo."

Jaquelin glanced at Philippe.

"He's right. It is a little Indiana Jonesy."

"Yes…" Philippe said licking his lips. "But! We get to mix in any flavor we want!"

"French-Vanilla? Butter-Pecan? Chocolate-Deluxe?"

"Anything you want my sweet-toothed hermano."

"I'd go for red berries myself. Makes more sense, culinary speaking." Meth said absently, the blood rushing to his head making him forget he was dinner. "But you do you."

He'd been hanging for twelve hours. It was a miracle of sheer will that he hadn't passed out again. But he was becoming incoherent. They needed to operate now, and they had to catch the brain before it hit the floor.

"Alright." Philippe said. "Do you have the pizza cutter?"

"Yup." Jaquelin answered. "But it's gonna take time."

"Hand it over." Philippe said eagerly. "Think about it: Brain…Sorbet."

Jaquelin tossed him the pizza cutter, and Philippe approached an incoherent and babbling Method Man with a smile worthy of a four year-old's first taste of frozen yogurt.

"He was right." Jaquelin said, licking the back of the spoon. "Berries are better."

"If you think so, why you gotta eat all the Cookies and Cream too?" Philippe said, snatching one of the different colored bowls away from Jaquelin. Meth hung from the hook, his eyes frozen, the top half of his skull missing. Small bits of brain hadn't quite blended with ice cream, and made squishy sounds as Jaquelin gobbled up the brain sorbet in a mad rush for brain freeze. "Just stick to the Cherry Garcia you hungry bastard."

The strange wave of Wu-Tang related disappearances has come to a tragic revelation when the dead bodies of Inspectah Deck - Jason Hunter, and Raekwon - Corey Woods, were found at a recording studio in Harlem.

Forensics officers have concluded that Raekwon was also cannibalized. Four more bodies were found ridden with bullets, while Method Man - Clifford Smith, confirmed to have been in the recording studio at the time, is still missing.

The police assume that Masta Killa – Jamel Arief, Ghostface Killah, - Dennis Coles and U-God – Lamont Hawkins are likely dead or kidnapped. An investigation is underway.

"We're now quite certain, we are witnessing an ancient ritual, involving the passing of energy from one being to another through means of consumption. While we believed that the profanation at the Ol' Dirty Bastard - Russell Jones', grave was an act of vandalism,

we are now inclined to tying it into this wave of tragic, and frankly gross, occurrences."

If you're one of the living members of the Wu-Tang Clan, or Wu affiliates you are advised to report to the nearest precinct as soon as possible. For your sake, and Hip-Hop's.

Akhbar Levenstein Jr. reporting for CNN.

"They gotta be expecting us." Jaquelin said wearily, walking down the dark steps to the underground studio where RZA and GZA were rumored to be hiding. It paid to be on the inside now that they were building a rep.

"Everybody expects death, bruh. And no one sees it coming." Philippe replied.

"The whole WORLD knows. What if we got the 411 so they could bust us? This whole thing reeks of a trap. I mean come on, man; we're about to blow up. Why you gotta fiend for more flesh, dawg?"

Jaquelin was right, but Philippe would never admit it. He would eat his way through the Wu, then Mobb Deep, and then kill Kanye just for kicks. He was hungry.

They walked down the staircase for an hour, then two.

"Something is off." Jaquelin said. "We should be in Australia or have struck oil by now."

"It's all good." Philippe said, but he didn't sound as assured as usual. "There's a faint light down there, you'll see it soon."

They descended for another half hour before the light revealed a room, with the hint of a beat coming through the door.

"Quiet." Philippe said. "We want to get them clean and quick."

"And then drag the bodies all the way back up?"

"Na. We can eat them dead and raw. Makes no difference anymore, we're strong enough. Now shut up."

They stood by the door, breathed in, and then threw themselves inside.

Two figures sat on throne-like chairs, the light behind them blinding Jaquelin and Philippe slightly, but also delineated the two forms clearly enough for them to shoot true.

Two bullets hit the Ruler Zig-Zag-Zig Allah in the chest. Another two hit the God Zig-Zag-Zig Allah in the head. The lights went out before a purple glimmer, growing from the chairs, surrounded the bodies that hadn't stumbled back, nor fallen, illuminating the room in a nauseating glow.

RZA pulled the bullets out of his chest. GZA winked at them and let the bullets roll inside his head and pulled them out of his mouth.

"Run!" Philippe screamed.

They ran for hours.

The door kept moving ahead of them every time they threatened to cross the threshold.

They finally turned around, and the two cousins were still sitting there, at the exact same distance no matter how fast and long they ran, smiling at them knowingly, their wounds healed.

"You've now entered the 36th Chamber," GZA said quietly.

They turned to face RZA and GZA.

"How?" Philippe screamed.

"Told you it was a set-up." Jaquelin said shaking, every word marked by clicking teeth.

"Wu-Tang is forever." Bobby Digital responded with a smooth smile on his lips. "We shouldn't tell you, but since you won't be telling anybody..." His smiled deepened. "And now, from the slums of Shaolin, introducing: Ol' Dirty Bastard, Inspectah Deck, Raekwon the Chef, U-God, Ghostface Killah, Masta Killa." All the dead members started walking out of a room behind the thrones as their names were called. "And the…."

"M-E-T-H-O-D Man!" Johnny Blaze toasted, stepping out last, triumph painted over his face, complete with a full skull and not a trace of sorbet.

Jaquelin hurled. Philippe inquired again.

"But HOW?" U-God grinned. "Our souls are in the thirty-five other chambers but yours will be ours. Yours will be in our music." The RZA rose from his chair, all nine members of the hip-hop legends closing in on the two terrified teens. "You wanted to make music history? You will."

And so it happened, the way new songs of the deceased Tupac would leak and appear; an old, blood red vinyl appeared at a record store in Staten Island with two new Wu-Tang Clan songs.

It was untitled but it had all its deceased members on the track.

The red vinyl was passed around to hip hop lovers around the world until Angie Miller of Hot 97 got a hold of the unnamed album to play to her fans.

She held the album in her left hand and got the record needle wit her right. "RIP Wu-Tang. Crazy though, cause they keep putting out jams. This is one of their best tracks, but I tell y'all, as I hold this, I feel something weird in this record. Maybe that's why no one will just own it… for those who haven't heard it, this is one of the most raw and brutal tracks I've heard by the Wu or by anyone. It's untitled, but I'mma call it the Slaughter Mill."

Angie placed it on the record player and pressed play.

Oh no. Philippe thought as the record spun, the diamond getting closer to his pressed form inside the vinyl. Closer to his face. Oh no.

The beat started banging, the diamond cut into his eyes, chopping into his brain with every turn of The Slaughter Mill, slicing his tongue, crushing his teeth to powder as his lacerated soul bled inside the disk.

She flipped the disk over.

Pressed play.

It was Jaquelin's time to scream.

62

5

Jeremy Thompson

WU-TANGIBLE

"**B**eyond the slums and dark hills, the shrines and the *impenitentiaries*, the poison ivy pillars and the thousand mortuaries, there exists a sacred site," the elder said. "There, the foundations of reality shuddered, as deities clashed. The future was assured, at great cost." Dressed in sacerdotal vestments, thrumming with moon glow, he regarded me with eyes that had seen past the cosmos.

He was the most aged among us, and the wisest.

Of his younger years, there were stories. "A priest," some attested. "An assassin," declared others. "Those pursuits aren't always mutually exclusive," a few reminded.

"Are you speaking mythology?" I asked, as stars flowed across the black sky, fertilizing the dusky cell that would sprout into morning's zygote. "Extraterrestrial pyramids obliterated by purple rays, shit like that?"

"To those who've escaped the ignorance-mongers to become truly awakened, mythology becomes mathematics," the elder said. Remembering sad saxophones, the husky vocals of a songstress, and the thump-ba-dump-thump underlying 'em, I nearly understood him.

"So can I visit the site as some sorta spiritual sojourn? Do relics remain: fragments of stained glass saucers and futuristic science?"

"What remains within those shifting dimensions cannot be spoken of," he answered. "There are metaphysics at play there that can only be experienced in person, by those pure of intention. Indeed, the eyes of gods are upon us, and I can say little else."

"With all due respect, sir, how can I learn the truth of your assertion? How might I visit this place without directions?"

"The route is not mine to impart," the old man intoned. "If you wish to visit that site, watch the constellations until they reconfigure. If your heart remains uncorrupted, a celestial map will shine for you."

With that, he strode into the pitch-black, into circumstances I'm unable to relate, having never seen him again.

Seven years later, the stars finally moved for me.

Hell had found my tenement, portended by a mask of Renaissance mahogany nailed to its front entrance. Carved from a dead man's casket, it meant that a truce had been shattered. There'd be no mercy granted, no shortage of lead. Already, my downstairs neighbor had been found with her throat slit.

After dropping my three-year-old son off at his mother's—where he'd remain for the foreseeable future—I went to see some men about firearms, to purchase off-the-books. Though I owed no allegiance to the thugs in my building, their enemies had become mine through proximity. I needed to be ready for these bastards. They wouldn't enter my apartment while I drew breath.

In a strip mall parking lot, well past closing time, I watched a Jeep Wrangler pull up and expel five men. They wore military fatigues, bulky with body armor underlying 'em. These men were not to be messed with, so I flashed a bag of hundreds as a preamble.

"You goin' to war?" I was asked, as we regarded each other from opposite sides of pale parking space lines.

And so I told them my story, and received an answer most unexpected, "In battle, your allies must be pure of intent. By your own admission, you fight alongside snakes. Do you think their fangs won't stick you in the end?

"Now, a private army can be hired, and you can put those boys in your building and their armed opponents in the dirt. If you're interested, add another zero to that sum and dial us back."

Into the Jeep they piled, to rumble back into the night. Wondering where those grim fellows had arrived from and where they were headed, I slowly sat down on the blacktop. Shards of beer glass crunched beneath me. A cat yowled in the distance, then it was shot.

Please have mercy, I prayed to an indifferent deity, knowing that I had no more cash to distribute, and nowhere else to reside.

And lo, I heard a breakbeat, possessed of no earthly origin. Glancing to the dark firmament, I saw constellations in motion: Pisces, Aquarius and Scorpio merging to form the contours of roads I knew well. Around them, the remaining constellations gathered, becoming stadiums and other landmarks.

Escaping the impending violence, I hopped into my ride and drove outta Beast Bellyville.

Months passed with me living out of that vehicle, using my bag of cash to buy gas, meals, and other necessities. Speaking only to waitresses and sales clerks, I felt years of accumulated disdain deteriorate to dust within me. Hearing no negativity, I hummed to myself.

By day I drove. Nights found me watching the heavens, to see the next day's journey illuminated. The countryside sprouted slums and shed them, then did it again and again. Hearing sirens, I ignored 'em. Burnt skeletal, abandoned vehicles loomed. Approached by peddlers and prostitutes, I retained my funds.

Finally, as I breathed into cupped hands to fight hypothermia, on the coldest night that I've ever experienced, my constellation route sprouted a destination point: the bright star Polaris, most divine. Its corresponding earthly location would be reached in the morning.

Fog ruled the Earth, it seemed. Swallowing all visibility, it rendered everything unbroken grey, purgatorial. Though a collision could've ended my trek at any moment, I drove until an almost deafening, buzzing sonance filled my skull.

Emerging from my car, I found that what I'd taken for blacktop was scorched soil—cracked, threaded with blades of dead grass. There were spent bullet casings in all directions, amid craters and twisted shrapnel. There were discarded blades and firearms, weathered rusty. "The sacred site," I whispered with all due reverence. "I've found it."

Ahead, bees swarmed, so firmly clustered that they seemed a wall when fog-obscured. Below them, a carpet of corpses attested to millions of stings. Some were skeletons; others were putrefying, purple-blotched, and bloated. "Killer bees," I said to myself while approaching.

The buzzing was so omnipresent, it made my teeth vibrate. Other sounds hid within it: guitar riffs and record scratches.

Knowing that my life could be extinguished, I stepped amidst the lethal insects. Surging into my clothing, they met every inch of my skin with their fuzzy physicalities. I felt wings, abdomens, legs, and mandibles brushing my skin, yet not a single stinger punctured me. Shades of yellow, black and brown filled my eyes, as I trudged forward.

Carefully, I stepped through the swarm with my

mouth closed and my eyes squinting like I was stoned. Pure of purpose, I trod upon human corpses, wondering if I'd soon eternally slumber amongst them. Ribs crunched beneath my heels; teeth tumbled to the soil.

As that perilous, buzzing multitude lessened in density, I glimpsed freestanding suits of ō-yoroi armor in the corners of my sight. Built of lacquered leather and iron, they flanked me, with fearsome oni-faced masks sneering beneath their tiered helmets. Though unoccupied, they stood as if adorning noble samurai, gripping swords sharp enough to bisect fleas. *Are they moving?* I wondered, accelerating my steps.

Uninjured, I emerged from the ranks of the bees. Even the clothes-invading insects returned to the swarm.

I gasped, beholding the supernatural. A steaming pond, its waters eerily green, hazed the physiques of those floating above it. Numbering ten, they stood upon air. Though they wore human forms, the static electricity they exuded attested to otherwise. Feeling it at a distance, I hesitated to step closer. But cowardice might have meant my death.

Crouching at the edge of the water, I peered past the steam to see speakers, iPods, microphones and Technics. All of them submerged. They appeared undamaged, as if the water barely touched them. Heaped, they almost reached the pond's surface.

"Raise your eyes," a gravelly voice demanded, each syllable a casket creak. The mist thinned enough for me to distinguish physical features, and I almost recognized the ten levitators, but I had never encountered them before.

The man addressing me wore four pointed rings

upon his right hand, sharp enough to punch-shred faces, and gold fangs on his teeth, jagged enough to chew souls. "I am the Resurrector," he said. Indicating his nine compatriots in turn, he named: "He is the Genius, and he is the Pillager. He is the Chef, and beside him, the Inspector. There stands the Man of Iron, with the Killer on his left." An animated figure was the Unique Son. The Blazing Man exhaled smoke rings as his head sprouted flames, feeling not even a pain twinge. The last of them, the Golden Armed, wore kote made of that precious metal. "The city cries," he intoned, and I nodded.

"Are you ghosts?" were the words that I spoke, when I found my voice.

"Ghosts arise from the corporeal," answered the Genius.

"Our origins are strictly digital," said the Resurrector.

The Inspector expounded: "We began as digital bit streams, to be precise, units of information communicated over the Internet, absorbed into phones and iPods to deliver music to ears. Our fathers spat lyrics into microphones, unaware that the millions of ears that found 'em, and minds that pondered 'em, were enough to believe us into being."

"I was the first," said the Resurrector, "digitalized vocals that attained knowledge of self. My essence streamed into a singularity that spat me onto the mortal plane. Everywhere, I saw sickness and devilishment, and so I brought forth my clansmen to combat it.

"After our fathers ascended, music committed hari-kari. Ignorance and incompetence were celebrated until nobody cared anymore. True talent was ignored until it perished." Motioning toward a pile of leather-bound tomes beyond the pond, he intoned, "The time has arrived to bring it back to life. Behold the word unspoken."

"The uncontrollable substance," echoed the Inspector.

"We awaited one worthy," said the Killer. "Pretenders arrived, snakes in human form, wishing to corrupt the message. Beneath bees they crumpled, to rot without honor."

"Be worthy," said the Resurrector, and then the ten men were gone.

Making a makeshift sack of my parka, I transported the 36 Manuals from that site. Crushing the honorless dead to the soil, I re-entered the bee swarm, and emerged unstung once again.

Day and night, I now read, assimilating the knowledge supreme. Soon, I will share what I've learned with those ready to listen.

A rebirth is on the horizon; it echoes into my dreams as I slumber. Raw enough to make heads bounce.

The real music is returning.

6

Jeff C. Carter

ABBOT OF THE WHITE LOTUS

邵氏兄弟（香港）有限公司)
IN
SHAW {SB} SCOPE

PRODUCED BY:
RUN RUN SHAW

Kami kept her hood up and long black hair over her face as she passed the corner where the local tong slung dimebags of White Lotus. A skinny black teen with cornrows and a hook sword hung from the waist of his saggy jeans whistled, "Yo, shorty!" She ignored him and continued down the bloodstained sidewalk to the ivory steps of the Lotus Clan temple.

The towering Chinese temple stood regal and immaculate among the graffiti wrapped tenements, neon lit pawnshops and burnt-out row houses. Kami sneered at the deception. The temple was not above the corruption, it was the source. The abbot was a drug lord, and his name was Pai Mei. His kung fu cartel controlled the flow of White Lotus, the narcotic powder that turned users into fighters and addicts into deadly maniacs.

Lotus Clan assassins had taken the lives of her

parents with a sword. The drug had taken her twin brother's life with a syringe. This would be her final assault on the White Lotus Clan. She had nothing else to lose.

A pair of monks in blue robes guarded the golden doors and stared at her with suspicion. Japanese folks rarely strayed from Little Hiroshima and knew better than to approach Lotus Clan turf. Once, she had strutted past these guards in a stolen schoolgirl outfit. For all their contempt of the Japanese, the guards had been eager to woo her. She had surprised them with her tiger style, only to be later crushed by the abbot. Pai Mei let her live, but she would never again pass as an innocent girl.

The words from her father's manual whispered in her mind. *Every deity and the spirits of your dead comrades are watching you intently. Just before collision, it is essential you do not shut your eyes and miss the target.*

Kami swept back her hood and hair revealing her scar-lined face and black eyepatch. If the guards recognized her, it was too late. Her katana swept across their throats and they tumbled down the stairs gurgling blood.

She pushed open the doors and charged into the darkness beyond. The stairs rose like an ivory dragon, making her dizzy with déjà vu and dread. The marble edges that snapped her bones and cracked her teeth were sharp as ever. The waterfall of blood she spilled, first from her ruined eye socket and later from a severed leg, had been scrubbed clean. The stairs were ready for a final trip down to the gutter and hell below.

She crested the top and hit a narrow room lined with stone bodhisattvas. The statues faced a huge crimson idol of Guan Yu, the Saint of War. Kami screamed into his wrathful face. "Pai Mei!"

In her first assassination attempt, she had relied on the strength of her kung fu. That had cost her an eye and a long trip down the stairs, ears ringing with Pai Mei's cruel laughter. He had dangled her bloody eye and called out, "Come back and we will see if you are stronger."

She had licked her wounds in her empty apartment in Little Hiroshima. Beneath her parent's bed, buried in her father's WWII uniform and medals, she found grandfather's katana. The rich deer suede wrapping of the handle felt at home in her hands. The rough ray skin locked into her grip, extending her will with balanced steel and a razor's edge. She had been sure this would be the instrument of her revenge.

She snapped back to the present when a dozen gold robed monks spilled from behind the statues, eyes glazed over and fingers twisted into crane beaks. She cut them down like bamboo saplings. More arrived to churn the air with slender swords. Their flexible blades yielded to her hardened katana, followed by their flesh and bones.

She limped over slaughtered monks and behind Guan Yu's blood spattered grin. She parted a beaded curtain with the tip of her sword to reveal a swank lounge beyond. Her heavy artificial leg landed softly in white shag carpet. Flat screen televisions flickered along her blade.

Grandfather's katana had taken her far in her second raid on the temple, yet her fate had been sealed. Clinging to her wretched life had strangled her fighting spirit with fear. Every junkie she fought was a reminder of her twin brother's overdose.

She did not find Pai Mei's inner chamber. The abbot found her. That day she learned the true power of the White Lotus. The old priest had ingested the drug in its purest form for so long that his entire body was infused with qi. He laughed as he shifted his 'vital nerve' from her penetrating sword. No matter how fast or how deep she struck, he remained invincible.

He had plucked the sword from her cramped, blood-slick hand and hacked off her left leg at the knee. When he threw her down the stairs the second time, he tossed the sword but kept the leg. "Come back and face me again, if you can conquer the stairs!"

While she bled through her bandages and dirty sheets back home, she rifled once more through her father's war souvenirs. She found a rusted steel canister on a wooden stick, an old type 98 fragmentation grenade. She unscrewed the detonator cap and fished out the brittle fuse string, eager to end a lifetime of futile suffering.

The shutters blew open and a divine wind roared through the squalid room, tearing the cover off a yellowed book titled *Tokkōtai Shudō*. This was the Imperial Japanese Army's manual for suicide pilots. It became her new *Art of*

War, Book of Five Rings and Holy Bible. It was her salvation, and it would be her revenge.

Kami entered the lounge and startled a group of half-naked women reclining by a fireplace. They let out a chorus of shrill screams, but the only monk in the room, a DJ in a fur robe and chunky headphones stooped over his turntables, oblivious. A pacing white tiger on a long gold chain sniffed the bloody sword and its whiskers bristled. The girls fled, stumbling as their stiletto heels snagged in shag carpet.

The tiger snarled and pounced, claws outstretched and jaws drooling. It reached the end of the gold chain and was snapped back to the floor. The DJ shrieked and bolted, yanking his headphones free. A gritty track blasted from the sound system, flooding the room with chattering horns, violent beats and the gritty, relentless voices of eight men.

A crew of tattooed roughnecks with long single braids and thick iron bracelets rolled into the lounge. The largest had '187' emblazoned on his swollen chest and a face like a cinderblock with a mustache. He pointed at Kami.

"Hey girl, we're going to teach you a lesson."

Kami sneered, "A lesson in what?"

He crossed his hands and curled his fingers into claws. "In tiger style!"

Kami kicked a leather chair at him and he gutted it with his hooked fingers. She thrust her katana through the cloud of stuffing.

He deflected the blade with his iron bracelet and spun, gouging a set of deep tracks across her stomach. Kami stumbled back in shock.

The others closed in like walls of glistening muscle. She was trapped in a tornado of vicious claws all blurring the air in search of her arteries. Her desperate swings rang off their bracelets as each man stripped the fabric and skin from her body.

The brute with the mustache reared back his bloody hand. "Your sword is useless! Do you want to bleed to death, or should I end your misery?"

Kami remembered the words of the manual. *Transcend life and death. When you eliminate all such thoughts, you can disregard your earthly life.*

She threw her sword across the room. It landed with a soft clink.

The white tiger sprang from its broken chain and fell upon the men like a buzz saw. A few iron bracelets rang off its massive claws but their chimes were drowned out by the guttural death cries and satisfied roars.

Kami plucked her katana from the shag carpet and left the tiger to its feast.

She padded down a hallway to a set of plastic tarp draped doors. Through a small window she could see the lab where children in cheap respirators stood at a long table, sorting White Lotus and packing it into bricks. Kami tied off her wounds with strips of fabric from her shredded clothes and saved a large piece to wrap around her mouth and nose.

She pushed opened the doors and hurried past the

jostling, powder-frosted children. Their eyes darted about, tracking her sword, movement, stance and breathing. White Lotus seeped into their bloodstreams despite the masks, and soon Pai Mei would put them on the streets as disposable weapons. Kami wanted the abbot dead before that happened.

The door on the far side of the lab crashed to the ground in a plume of dust. A whip-thin bald man with wild eyes entered. The dust thinned, revealing more and more scars on his taut, wiry flesh. He cleared the cloud with a powerful gust from his hand. There were chunks of branded flesh on his arms and legs seared into the forms of animals: a tiger, dragon, crane, leopard, snake, mantis, monkey, hawk, and so on, every style of kung fu she'd ever heard of. The beasts were separated by track marks, deep pits dug by needles used to mainline White Lotus.

Kami leapt backwards onto the table, her fake leg nearly buckling beneath her. She aimed her sword at the kung fu maniac's face. His scarred features were so distorted by fury that his race was impossible to determine. Kami wondered what those bulging eyes saw; a woman, an enemy, a diagram of pressure points to be destroyed?

She kicked a brick of White Lotus and split it horizontally, directing the spray with the flat of her blade. The powder shot at his eyes, followed by the katana.

Her sword froze in midair. The powder had struck its mark and blinded him, but he had still caught the blade between his palms.

He used the trapped blade to jab her in the face with the butt of her own sword. She tripped and landed on her back. Only an instinctive roll saved her from a hammer fist that smashed the table in half.

Kami spilled to the floor in a heap of broken wood, drugs and sweaty children. The kids scurried away as the maniac stalked through the dust, sucking White Lotus through flared nostrils. Thick throbbing veins strained against his scars.

She feinted left and rolled past him. He drove her back with a kick to the chest. His flat hands probed the air, slithering like snakes. She gasped for breath and his ear's twitched, honing in on every sound.

She crept backwards to the lounge.

Her limping steps were muffled by the shag carpet, her movements buried by the hip-hop thumping from the speakers. She aimed her sword and smiled. Then she remembered the tiger.

The hunched predator lifted its dripping jaws from a man's abdomen, its snow white fur splattered scarlet. The tiger's pale blue eyes focused past her. The maniac entered and tilted his head, entranced by the music.

The tiger roared a challenge and pounced. The maniac leapt without hesitation to meet it half way.

Kami's jaw hung slack, awed by his fighting spirit.

The tiger hooked its claws into the scarred man's back, but he kept it rigid as iron. His crane technique pierced the tiger's blue eyes. It yowled and sought his jugular in return. He relented to its crushing weight and rolled, using his legs to thrust the wounded animal into the fireplace. The tiger roared and bucked him through the air.

Kami's sword was waiting. She drove it through his stomach and out his back. An agonized moan escaped, but it was only the tiger. The maniac lifted her and flung her back into the lab.

Kami's nose smashed onto the powder covered floor. She clamped her mouth tight and tried not to breathe. The scarred man jumped and aimed a stomp at her head.

She shoved herself backwards and snatched the protruding handle from his stomach. It ripped free with a spout of blood and he collapsed to his knees. She rose and torqued her hips, bringing the blade down in a decapitating stroke.

She saw the brick of White Lotus leave his hand too late. It hit the edge of her sword and exploded, filling her open mouth. She gagged and clamped her throat shut to keep from swallowing.

The scarred man sprang up and opened his bloodshot, powder encrusted eyes. He batted aside the sword and drilled her neck with a flurry of mantis style strikes. The wet lump of powder slid into her stomach and lungs.

A peal of laughter floated in the dusty air. Her quivering eyes looked up into the cruel face of Pai Mei. His wispy eyebrows and beard blurred into the white powder that had poisoned her and everything she knew. He tossed his beard over his shoulder in a dismissive gesture and swept from the room, his white silk robe whispering behind him.

The scarred man snapped a kick into her heaving back and sent her flying. She barely maintained her grip on the sword or avoided impaling herself as she sprawled.

She landed in a tranquil sea of green. The temple's

inner chamber was a massive hydroponic farm, its endless rows of tanks burgeoning with white lotus flowers. Pai Mei stood in the center of the greenhouse and Kami realized that his white robes, long beard, large wispy eyebrows and top knot were all parts of that same rare flower.

She shook her head to fight off the hallucination but her vision grew sharper. She could perceive the branches of his nervous system glowing with qi energy like the thousands of plants floating around them. Embers of qi energy caught flame and rolled through her own body.

"Did you ever question why I spared you?" Pai Mei laughed. "I wanted to see if you were as strong as your brother."

Kami pushed herself to her feet. "What about my brother?"

He laughed again. "Has your lost eye left you completely blind?"

The scarred man stalked in, gripping his stomach with one hand and licking White Lotus powder from the other. Kami looked beneath the scars and blood and saw the shadow of her lost brother's face.

"Kaze?"

She reached out to him. He caught her wrist and dislocated her right arm with a wet crunch. Kami clutched her arm and screamed.

"Your brother craved the power of the White Lotus," Pai Mei said. "With one taste, he became addicted, consuming amounts that would kill a normal man. Recovering from overdoses that made him even stronger. I offered him an unlimited supply of pure Lotus if he would serve me. To test his loyalty, I asked him to kill your parents."

She focusing on the pain to block out the memory of her parent's brutalized bodies.

Pai Mei roared with laughter. "Imagine my delight when you found your way to us? Now we shall see; which one of you has grown stronger?"

Kami stared into her brother's red eyes. Nothing reflected in his gaping black pupils. He was dead inside, as gone as their parents. She would avenge them all.

She swung her sword with one hand towards the abbot. Kaze's leg shot towards her face. She released the katana. The kick smashed her through a glass tank and drenched her in swampy water.

Pai Mei looked down at the pool of crimson spreading down his white silk robe. The katana stuck from his ribs, quivering in time with his heartbeat. Blood dribbled from the priest's mouth even as its corners twisted into a smile. "Fool. I can shift my vital nerve at will. No single blow can kill me!"

He clapped his palms against the blade and ejected it from his torso. It clattered to the floor. Kaze dragged her by the hair to Pai Mei. The abbot latched onto her neck with an eagle claw. His face danced with delight as he crushed out her life.

Kami popped her arm back into socket and gently pressed her palm to Kaze's heart. He flinched, expecting an attack, and then froze. Her qi pulsed in sync with his own. Their life energies reflected like mirrors.

His dry lips trembled, voice rusty from lack of use. "Sister?"

"Soon you will be unique," Pai Mei chuckled. "You

shall-urghkk!"

The abbot dropped Kami and turned, revealing a chunk of silk and flesh gouged from his back. Kaze's arm was flexed and dripping fresh blood.

Kami grabbed her katana and thrust it deep into Pai Mei's stomach.

"We can beat him together!"

Kaze flailed at Pai Mei with a windmill of tiger claws. The abbot gracefully floated out of reach. Kami tried to blindside him with a kick but he bent backwards, sending Kaze's talons ripping across her real leg. The siblings crashed in a heap of sweat and blood.

"Your kung fu is still no match for me," Pai Mei dragged the sword from his stomach, "and your sword technique is childish." He threw the katana across the greenhouse. It vanished with a distant splash.

Kami stared into her brother's eyes. They were softening to something human, and he was pale from blood loss. She touched his scorching forehead and whispered the final words from the suicide manual. *"You must use your full might for the last time in your life. Exert supernatural strength."*

They helped each other up. Kaze pushed a purple bulge of intestine back into his open stomach. Kami leaned on her fake leg and tested her balance. The abbot lifted his chin imperiously and tossed his wispy beard over his shoulder.

The twins attacked together, angling to cut off

all escape. Even when their blows connected, they could not find the shifting vital nerve. Pai Mei punished them for each false move, crushing ribs with gnarled fists and rupturing organs with lightning-quick palm strikes.

Kaze slipped in his own blood and collapsed.

Pai Mei's arm coiled back. His lean bicep tensed and his clawed fingers darted towards Kami's eye like the beak of a carrion bird.

Remember when diving into the enemy to shout at the top of your lungs. At that moment, all the cherry blossoms of Yasukuni Shrine will open for you.

She caught his arm, hoisted herself up and drove her fake leg deep into his groin.

The abbot clamped down with his thighs, trapping it far inside his crotch. "That is not where I keep my vital nerve," he laughed. He hammered a blow straight down that popped her fake leg from its stump.

The string ripped free from the fragmentation grenade hidden inside the leg.

Kami screamed, *"Ikken hissatsu!"*

Kaze recognized the Japanese phrase, 'Annihilate with one blow.'

Pai Mei's gloating eyes grew wide when he saw the look of triumph on her face. He sucked in his breath and ejected the leg towards Kami.

Kaze tackled the abbot, pinning the grenade between their bodies. They erupted in a red flash, shattering the hydroponic tanks and greenhouse walls.

Kami rubbed glass from her eye. Her brother's body floated by, his face serene at last.

Pai Mei gurgled, still standing in the rising water.

Blood poured from a hundred wounds and spattered the White Lotus flowers swirling around him.

"You struck my vital nerve…with…one blow…," he said until he could no longer stand and splashed to his death face down in the bloody water.

7

Loren Kleinman

SUNSHINE

I'm out of matches.

I've been waiting for her to come home for hours, and I've done everything to keep my mind off of her dimpled thighs, her skin. I'm trying hard to avoid thinking about her wide eyes as I go down on her, her fingers through my hair.

I keep searching for matches, for her.

She used to keep them in a small brass container on the top of the fireplace. But they're not there. Not a single one. Nothing in its place, not her books stacked on the dining room table, or her comb, knotted with black hair. The dog isn't here either — just his battered toys and torn socks.

I've called her at least ten thousand times. A lash to my back each time she doesn't pick up.

If she picked up, I'd tell her: "My love is a hummingbird sitting that quiet moment on the bough, as the same cat crouches." I'd tell her "love is hazardous," "love is sunshine," "love is all I need to get by." I'd tell her to just let me talk, not explain anything. I'd tell her my love is the remainder of the world, it's a slammed door, and I'm drunk as shit wondering where all my luck went.

I think of the garden. The one we made together in the back of the house. The big white rock still by the bird pond. That night we almost woke the shitty neighbors.

"You stay right here," she said.

She stood over me, her naked body, hard and soft and creased in the right places. Her face, vulnerable, as she picked up bunches of grass and spread them all over my chest. She walked over to the large rock, under the darkness and danced for me as my phone played "You're All I Need." I loved when she bent over and I could see her soft, deep-rooted pussy. I could get off just watching her.

"You like it like this, huh?" She danced.

"You know I do, Sunshine."

"Am I your only Sunshine?"

"More vicious than anyone."

"What do you mean?"

"I love you, but you're crazy," I said. "You're doomed."

"You like Bukowski more than any other girl I know."

"Listen," I said. "I drove up north expecting not to find love, but then I met you and I said I couldn't promise you anything, I'll bore you, and then what did you do?"

"I said relax." She continued to dance and lifted her leg on the rock.

I watched her like she was some place I remembered, like she was someone I knew in another life. She didn't mind me watching her, me looking straight through her. She didn't mind. She was my Sunshine.

"I love you," I said.

"Just watch me."

"I can't keep my eyes off you."

"I'm bright Sunshine. I'm warm Sunshine. And now I'm going to ride you hard," she said.

She walked away from the rock, and looked down at me, let her wild hair fill the open space around her head. She reached down for the whiskey.

"I'll do the drinking. You just recite me some Ibsen or some shit like that."

I loved the way she shook, so many fingers in the air, so many toes wiggling into the damp ground.

"Why, why, why, why?" she yelled.

"Why, what?"

"There's never enough time to dance for you."

She lit up a cigarette and the candles smoked around us. The dog just watched from his corner of the yard. We seemed to have it all. And we took it.

I looked out the window and still no sign of Sunshine. I went into the shower. Stripped down to my skin and sat in the tub. I wanted her to walk through the door so much, so much, so much. I'd give my mind to a demon to have her back.

Sunshine. Sunshine. Sunshine. I wish you were here.

Nothing is simple, and I remember when it happened.

"I'm dying," she said.

The rain came down. Her hands held her gut.

"You're not dead, yet."

"Not yet, but I'm going to die. It's in my stomach."

She held me on the sidewalk, next to the green and yellow houses, the gladiolas all-fresh.

"My luck is not so good right now," she said.

"What do you mean?" I cried.

"I mean no more hairpins on the table, no more stacked books, no more gardens."

"I don't want to know anyone else," I said. "How much time do we have?"

"It doesn't matter," she said.

"That's all that matters."

I open my eyes. She isn't here. I can still feel the rain, I can still smell her and the gladiolas.

I'm going to keep calling until she picks up.

The water is cold now. I get out and put on her yellow robe. No matter who I'm with next I'll always wear this robe; I'll always wear her hair pins and read her books.

"What are you laughing at?"

"You have mustard on your nose," she said. "Let me lick it off."

Sunshine stuck out her tongue.

"Stop, I'm saving it for later," I said. "Let's paint the walls."

"Right now?"

"Yea. They look so drab, like they were painted by a lonely person."

She cuddled up to me on the couch and rested her head on my shoulder.

"How lonely?"

"Who?"

"The person. How lonely do you think the person was?"

"Very. Like gravel pit lonely."

She laughed, sounded like a sun shower against a window. Like a horn on its last blow.

"Where do you come up with these lines?"

"Like can't-go-to-sleep lonely."

"You're crazy. You're doomed," she said and laughed.

"You're doomed." I turned to her. "Fucking beautifully doomed."

I breathed in the coconut oil on her skin.

"Stop breathing on me like that," she said.

"I'm gonna breathe on you for a long time."

I buried my mouth in her ear, and pushed the newspapers off the couch. I became silent over her.

"I don't dislike myself when I'm with you," I said.

"I like knowing these walls," she said.

Our eyes were the same eyes.

"Even though they were painted by a lonely person?"

"People are always worried about lonely people, about being alone," she said.

"Terrified," I whispered.

"You're secret is safe with me."

"You better not tell anyone," I said.

I held her down and stared at her: Her eyes. Her small wrists. I knew what Bukowski meant when he said "and this room is calm/so strange as if magic had become normal."

It was as high as we could get.

I'm calling her phone again. This time I'm leaving a message: "You finally got out by dying, leaving me with this awful present."

I've got to stop quoting Bukowski. I've got to stop drinking.

How wonderful the walls are after we painted them yellow, huh? And you're not here to stare at them with me. You're not here to keep my secrets.

And now the dog is barking outside, and I see some matches on the dresser next to your brush. And I miss you, Sunshine.

I can hear you walk, and whisper. I see that smile you smile and hear that laugh. I want to go to bed with you, but the ghost of you doesn't seem to care at all, you seem more interested in letting the dog in or finishing games of chess you'd always let me win. But that's what I like about you. It's what I miss about you. You were always what I needed and there for me.

And the words—they were never hard to say: I love you and always will.

8

Robert Dean

THE WORLD FELL BENEATH THE BROKEN CONCRETE

Beneath the broken concrete, the world fell. Toes gripped the insides of worn boots while the two shadows stared into one another – ready for war. This moment wasn't checkers, it was chess – it was a dedicated ritual to violence percolating at the tops of the lips of men, scratched into the void with a colorful name dabbed in blood.

The city moved at its usual speed – too fast for anyone to cool their heels. When in the limits of the urban wasteland, you watched every corner, every crack in the sidewalk, you looked for danger in the cobwebs and expected chaos to reign supreme despite maintaining breath. The city was covered in ash, dust and grime, but the cracks in the pavement were signatures against the years.

People sped along to destinations while others walked through the rooms of their houses, they ate dinner, they did natural human things. Some scheduled chaos into the night, while others scrawled sins across brick in spray paint – but right here, right now, this moment mattered to no one, but was laced with the fever of moment that equated the fate of this city. Even as the manicured blocks of affluence moved and shook at its volume, the dark markets still touched its shadows, only dressed in better clothes.

The night was cold. A freeze tickled the air, despite the rotten piles of snow caught between the voids of a beautiful reminder of nature, and a sad reminder of human progress as the snow grew filthy with dirt.

Knuckles cracked and for this moment, this attraction was poetic – everything within the archetype of humanity's mortal coil owed this breath, unknowingly to this scrawl of violence.

Counter clockwise, they walked, never allowing their eyes to slip off one another, for fear of pitiless blows raining down should one man make an unwise move. Hearts raced while sweat trickled down necks, lips and across shoulder blades, pooling along the lower back. Dust clouded up with each footfall, small chunks of concrete slathered their DNA through the air, hoping to land on fabric. Outside, past the shattered windows, through the air, a slight smell of burning wood trickled inward, most likely from the hobos along skid row burning a little of everything to keep warm on a bitter night such as this. The rats ran along the wires, and the world at large was unaware what hung in the balance.

The warriors kept their cool, their composure. Their adrenaline surged as ferocious winds swept down, crippling them with bursts of frigid tendrils scraping across their skin. The ether wanted them to know that despite their oath-sworn violence against one another, this fight belonged to the cosmos, being allowed but not celebrated by the old gods.

This moment existed because of the death of an elder – a murder of a statesman, a no-no amongst the tribes of the city. Despite the creed to outwit, outlast and outsmart one another at every turn, to kill an elder was forbidden. The mafia erased anybody in the way while these villains plotted moves against the traditions of the old ways.

As an unknown arrow swept through the window of his apartment, the elder dropped to his knees, blue in the face, red in the neck, as the projectile split his airway. This act of violence brought forth the war. And in the wake of this action, buildings burned, and bodies stacked.

The war had raged on. Waged behind the scenes, away from everyday citizens, but ask the pigs or anyone with a loved one in a dangerous part of town, and they'd inform you of the brutality splashed across the city's concrete. Bodies were found in bed, in alleys, even behind the counters at their shops, killed in the old ways: with piano wire, fists, knives, and tools of destruction. There were never any bullets – those were for the civilians. In this war, the colors you wore announced your flag to the neighborhoods, to the factions, and the world. You choose the color of your blood.

Bodies hung out of windows from Molotov cocktails thrown, leaving people to clean up the mess for supremacy. The battle flag stood tall against the skyline.

As their eyes searched one another, every sound in the distance or within feet echoed with a gravitas, a booming resonance that made their fibers stand on end. The warrior in yellow considered how to strike.

The man in black with the mask pulled tight around his eyes was his equal; every movement would lead to a reaction, so moves needed to be smart and precise. A simple leg kick couldn't be just that – simple. He had to allow himself enough time to spring back upon his heels should his aggressor move with fluidity.

The warrior in black wanted to kill. The bastard in yellow moved like a bee, his feet were too fast, almost – floating. Death could be the only triumph in this situation; he had to go for the neck. It was the only spot to land a crippling blow. If he landed a fist to the windpipe, there'd be a chance to knock him off his feet and move in with a strike equaling finality. The method had to be precise. The warrior in black's synapses fired, his heart raced, and his muscles ached, but his move would be swift, it would be righteous and maybe with luck, and skill, it would end the war.

Somewhere off in the distance, a ghetto blaster boomed through the empty streets, allowing its presence to be known from blocks away. While in the midst of the madness, sometimes, stealth wasn't the answer – it was all about vibrato. It was a call, a dare to come to arms. While trapped in battle, the warriors on the inside saw their lives amount to this moment, and on the outside the streets wanted an entirely different kind of reckoning with an ache for blood by trigger pulls, not fist falls.

The yellow warrior's fists bobbed up and down, acting as a pendulum to his burst waiting to explode in a fury of fists. His people, his family, his clan shot the arrow. It had to be done. They knew the consequence of betraying the laws of the old guard. He and his clan were hungry, weak and without facilities to thrive. They were hand to mouth, and without anything more than they could steal.

The black clan, on the contrary, had the best of all things, the breath of God at their backs, allowing for their dominance and successes on all fronts. By the death of the elder, the yellow clan announced their place in the world, and in the streets. And now, as bodies lined the morgues across town, it came down to this battle: the two most feared fighters in either arsenal meeting face to face.

The victor of this fight would be crowned as the new leader of the city's underground societies. And it would be his code, his doctrine, to which all others would subside.

There was struggle in their breaths. Every second spent not swinging was pushing and pulling the other to and from a position of power over one another. The balance was delicate. When they both dropped into this broken room, each warrior did his best to throw muscle behind his moves, trusting the years of training to execute movements with precision to destroy the opponent – the only problem was the two men were evenly matched. Their skills were a mirror image of one another, the two elite fighters of their clans, ready to kill, but put up against an enemy with a reactionary discipline.

The black warrior was the first to move, swinging his right hand around, and aiming toward the yellow warriors windpipe. Upon fast movement, the yellow warrior slid his left foot outward, sending each of them off balance. The black warrior steadied himself on his heels and the yellow warrior bounced back up on the balls of his feet.

In a quick succession, fists flew aiming to land anywhere. Each warrior moved like the ocean, the currents of their reactions, reflexes, and speed tested the waves of the ether.

Outside the building, the sound of footfalls grew louder. Boots marching echoed through the streets. A chorus was building. Two opposing sides descended upon the scene. The Battle Flag rose above the seas of men, women and children, ready to fight for their clans, their ideals. From a high-level view, the bodies looked like pismires spilling into an ant farm, looking to rebuild their lives after a child had shaken apart their work. From blocks away, they saw opposing colors, opposing lives.

But then the streams stopped, in front of the building housing the two finest warriors.

All it would take was a pin drop: ruckus was here.

9

Andy Rausch

THE NIGHT OL' DIRTY BASTARD CAME TO HOBOKEN

Kevin was pretty sure his life was over. He was as miserable as a man could ever be. He couldn't bear to stare down another day of depression and failure. It had all become too much. So here he was, sitting in the middle of the night on the side of a train bridge, his feet dangling down from up high. He'd been drinking Hennessy all evening, and he was pretty sure he was going to jump off this goddamn bridge and put an end to all his suffering.

There was nothing left to live for.

That he was wanting to off himself was no surprise to himself, and probably wouldn't have been much of a surprise to anyone who knew him.

Hell, he'd already tried once.

A long time ago.

When he was in high school Kevin drove his mother's old Station Wagon out to an isolated country road where there was no one there to see him end, or at least attempt to end, his crappy life. He started this little adventure by stretching a hose from the vehicle's exhaust pipe into the driver's side window. Then he sat there, listening to Kurt Cobain muttering to melancholy music, as the exhaust filled the car.

He started to cough and sputter, but death wasn't coming quickly enough, so Kevin tried a different approach. He got out of the car, feeling woozy as all hell, and wound up lying on the ground, sucking on the end of that hose. Now death would come with more urgency, he figured. What he didn't figure on, however, was the cop patrolling these back roads came upon him lying there, nearly unconscious, the hose dangling from his mouth like a near-spent cigar.

"What the hell you doing, boy?" asked the cop, shaking him.

Kevin was loopy and hadn't known what to say. The police officer assisted Kevin into the backseat of his car and took him on a little trip down to the cop shop. Kevin's father was called, and came down to the station to pick up his son. Kevin had been as embarrassed as he had ever been—perhaps even more embarrassed than the time his mother had walked in on his masturbating to the bras in a JC Penney catalog—and the conversation that had followed was a tough one. His father asked him why he would want to die, and Kevin divulged that he really had no friends to speak of. That he was bullied. That he hated life. This led to his father weeping in the car, and Kevin vowing to himself that he would never hurt his family this way again.

No more suicide attempts.

And yet here he was now, some twenty years after the fact, contemplating a swan dive off this bridge. Maybe, just maybe, he thought, a train would come along and save him the effort of leaping.

Kevin took another swig of the Henny and wept.

Kevin was not a religious man—he'd been raised the son of agnostics—but he now felt a prayer welling up from within his chest. "God," he managed. "Are you there?" Kevin looked up in the sky, but there was no response—not even a plane or a bird or even a cloud.

Nothing.

And again he asked, "Are you there, God?" But God said nothing. "I need your help if You're out there," he said, warm tears cascading down his cheeks. "I need you to show me if there's a better way."

But God remained silent.

Shit, Kevin thought. It was the same old thing—he wasn't going to receive any help or answers from the universe. And thus he concluded that there was no God. And to this, God replied, nothing.

Dammit.

So here he was, half-assedly drunk, sitting on the edge of this bridge, leaning more and more toward jumping to a sure death.

Again, he wept.

And then he heard a voice come from behind. A low, crazed voice, whose cadence carried a musicality unlike anything he'd ever heard.

"Kevin?"

Kevin turned and saw a black man standing

there behind him. The man had crazy jingle-jangle hair sticking up from his head like rays of sunshine in a child's crayon drawing. He was clad in a hoodie, baggy jeans, and Timberland boots.

The man took a step forward, and Kevin almost fell from his perch. He steadied himself.

"Who are you?"

Now Kevin saw the Wu-Wear logo on the man's shirt and the unlikely pieces began to shift into place. Kevin knew who this man was.

"Are you…Ol' Dirty Bastard?"

The man grinned, moonlight catching his gold teeth.

"You are, aren't you?"

The man nodded.

"But...you're...*dead.*"

"Do you believe in miracles, Kevin?"

"No."

"Can a mother fucker sit down."

Kevin nodded towards the spot beside him and said, "Of course."

Dirty sat down, dangling his Tims over the side of the bridge. "Can I have some of that Henny?"

Kevin handed him the bottle, and Dirty took a healthy swig.

"What is this?" asked Dirty. "Hoboken?"

"Yeah."

"I don't fuck with New Jersey."

"Why's that?"

"The women, son. The women here be crazy. I used to date a girl from Jersey. She had a big ol' fat butt.

Body was slamming, son. But she was—"

"Crazy?"

"Right," Dirty said, nodding in approval. "The girl was bonkers. You know, she tried to shoot my ass once. Threatened to shoot my balls off."

"Women are crazy."

"Exactly. You can't trust 'em."

Kevin agreed, thinking of his ex-wife.

"You can't get caught up in the power-u."

"Power-u?"

"The pussy, son," said Dirty. "You can't get caught up in all that. You can't even worry about that."

Kevin nodded, but said nothing.

Dirty grinned, his gold fronts glinting in the moonlight once again. "You already did, didn't you?"

"What?"

"Get caught up worrying about pussy."

Kevin nodded. "Yeah, I guess I did."

"You know what they say about fishes in the sea..."

"No," Kevin said. "What do they say?"

"Damned if I know, but they say some shit. Something about the little fishies in the sea...shitting on the waves."

Kevin just stared at him.

"So what's your problem, son?"

"I want to die."

"Trust me, life is good. I miss that shit everyday."

"So you're what? A ghost?"

"Yup," said Dirty. "I'm a motherfuckin' ghost, man."

Kevin was just drunk enough that this made sense

to him. "So why are you here?"

"To talk some sense into you, man."

"How exactly does all this work?"

"What do you mean?"

"I prayed to God, but instead of God, I get the ghost of O.D.B.?"

Dirty grinned again. "I'm a lot like God."

"How you figure?"

"Cause I'm the Big Baby Jesus, son."

Dirty took another swig.

"You know what this party needs?"

Kevin said he did not.

Dirty reached into his pocket and produced a Ziploc bag half filled with weed. "You wanna get high?"

Kevin laughed. "You're serious?"

"Hell, yes, I'm serious, son. I never joke about weed. We gonna smoke us a motherfuckin' blunt."

"You got one rolled?"

"Nah, but it ain't nuthin' but a thang. I'll roll us up a fat one. You just tell me what seems to be the problem, uh... What was your name again?"

"Kevin."

"Right. I'm shitty with names, son."

"Now what?" asked Kevin.

"You tell me about your problems."

"Well, first my Dad died this past year. That was real hard on me."

"I know," said Dirty.

Kevin's eyes narrowed. "You do?"

"Hell, yeah, I play cards with that motherfucker. And I'll tell you this much, he cheats."

Kevin's eyes got big. "You do? He does?"

"Hell yeah," said Dirty. "And you know what? That nigga still owe me $22!"

Kevin laughed. He didn't know what to say. Then, finally, he came up with something. "He ever mention me?"

"Sometimes."

"Oh yeah?"

"Yeah, we talk about our kids sometimes."

"What does he say?"

"Well, he's worried about your ass."

"He is?"

"Sure. Who do you think sent me here to talk to you?"

Kevin nodded.

"So why didn't he just come himself?" he asked.

To this, Dirty said, "Rules, man. They got rules up in Heaven. Your daddy couldn't come, so he sent me."

"My father sent Ol' Dirty Bastard to save my life?"

"Exactly." Dirty paused, paying extra attention to the spliff he was rolling. "I got cherry papers. You good with them."

Kevin smiled a shit-eating grin. "Sounds good to me. This is my favorite kind of weed."

Dirty looked at him, his mouth hanging open. "What kind is that?"

"The free kind."

Dirty chuckled. "Right, the free kind. You're right. That's the best kind."

"So you miss being alive, Dirty?"

"Man, I miss the pussy on earth."

"Aren't there women in Heaven?"

"Not the kind I like."

"What kind is that?"

Dirty grinned a big, silly grin. "Hoes, mufucka. I like hoes!"

"Hoes don't go to Heaven?"

"They do," said Dirty, "but they change their ways. They be actin' all uppity, like they got sticks up their asses."

"Word?" asked Kevin.

"Word."

"Is there sex in Heaven?"

"There is, but it's boring missionary sex."

"What kind of sex do you like?"

"Man, I miss doggie style. *A lot.*"

Kevin smiled, then took a swig.

"So what else is wrong?" asked Dirty.

"My wife left me."

Dirty nodded. "Yeah, I heard about that. She left you for one of them big-shot real estate agents."

"Yeah."

Dirty turned towards him, leaning in, getting right up in Kevin's face. "You wanna know something?"

"Sure."

"Dude's a homosexual."

"Who?"

"The guy your wife is with."

Kevin's eyes got big. "No shit?"

"No shit, son," said Dirty. "Dude's straight up gay."

"Will they stay together?"

"I don't know that. But I know he gay."

"How gay are we talking?"

"Liberace gay."

"That's pretty goddamn gay."

Dirty nodded.

"That actually makes me feel a whole lot better," said Kevin.

"I figured it would. You know what you need to do now?"

"What?"

"Get you some ass."

"But I thought you said pussy—"

"The *power-u*," Dirty interrupted.

"Right," said Kevin. "The power-u. I thought you said I shouldn't mess with that."

"Nah, man, you totally gotta mess with that."

"I do?"

"Yeah, but you don't wanna get tangled up in their drama. You just tap it and go."

Kevin asked, "Just like that?"

"Easy-peezy Japa-fuckin'-esey, son."

"Huh."

"What other problems you got?"

"I'm in debt."

Dirty laughed at this.

"What?" asked Kevin.

"Man, everybody's in debt."

"I'll bet you wasn't in debt."

Dirty's expression turned to a serious one. "You'd bet wrong, nigga."

"Really? But you were rich."

"You know how much child support I paid?"

"How much?"

"I got thirteen kids, man."

"So a lot?" asked Kevin.

Dirty nodded. "A lot." He held up the neatly-rolled blunt. "You wanna smoke this or what?"

"Hell yeah, I wanna smoke that."

"Let's do it then."

Dirty produced a Zippo lighter with a naked woman on its side. He put the blunt to his lips, lit it up, and inhaled deeply. Then, in a raspy voice, he said, "That shit is good, son." He passed the blunt to Kevin, who held it up and took a drag.

"So what else is troubling you?" asked Dirty.

"I spent the last seven years working on a novel, and apparently it sucks. It's been rejected by a whole slew of publishing houses."

"What's it about?"

Kevin hesitated.

"What?" asked Dirty.

"It's titled *Honkyland.*"

Dirty looked at him like he was crazy. "*Honkyland?*"

"Yeah, so what?"

"So nobody uses that word anymore—honky. Only old men say shit like that... Them cats from the seventies who was all militant and shit. Other than them, honky is about as dead as I am."

"Nobody says it?"

"Nope."

"Huh," said Kevin.

"So what's your novel about?" asked Dirty.

"It's about a white kid who goes to an all-black

college. It's about the trials and tribulations he faces because he's different."

"Goddammit, man," growled Dirty.

"What?"

"Niggas can't have anything. We can't even have all-black universities without white kids thinking they're entitled to go there."

Kevin thought about it. "So you think it's a bad idea?"

"Hell yeah, it's a bad idea." Dirty sat there for a moment. "Is this the first book you've written?"

Kevin said it was.

"Sometimes it takes a few times to get something right. Look at RZA... He had a record deal with Tommy Boy Records under the name Prince Rakeem before we started the Wu. And that shit bombed. But RZA didn't give up. He went back into the lab and went to work on some new shit. The same thing with GZA. He had an album called Words from the Genius on Cold Chillin' Records."

"And that was before Wu-Tang Clan?"

"Yeah, and again, it didn't sell. But he didn't give up. He went right back to work and came up with some new shit. And look at him today..." Dirty turned and looked at Kevin. "You still wanna kill yourself?"

"Well," Kevin said. "I do feel better."

"That's the weed."

"Nah, I think it was all the stuff you said."

Dirty nodded, taking another drag. "Cool, cool."

"Tell my Dad thank you."

"I'll do that shit," said Dirty.

They took turns passing the spliff back and forth, blowing thick clouds of smoke into the cool night air.

"I got a question that's totally off the subject," said Kevin.

"Yeah?"

"What contemporary rappers do you like?"

"Only the ones who were around when I was alive. Dudes like Jay-Z, Nas, Masta Ace, Sadat X, Everlast..."

"What do you think of these new cats?"

Dirty contemplated this as he took another drag from the spliff. "They all garbage, man. Every last motherfuckin' one of 'em."

"Really?"

"You like 'em?"

"Not really," admitted Kevin and took the spliff.

"Cool, you good," Dirty said as Kevin took a long drag.

When he looked over at where Dirty had been, he saw that the ghost had vanished. He looked around, but saw nothing.

"Dirty?"

But Dirty was gone—presumably back to playing cards with Kevin's dead father.

Kevin smiled and caught the first glimmers of the sun rising in the East.

Today was a new day.

Today would be a good day.

Kevin was going to live for many more.

10

Tom Leins.

INCARCERATED SCARFACES

Part 1: Demolished and Bruised

It was raining the day I arrived at Channings Wood. It suited my bleak mood.

On the prison bus I was handcuffed to a gangly white supremacist with facial hair like roadkill. He was a mouth-breather, and his breath smelled like a betting shop toilet. At least I got a fucking window seat.

I stared through the bulletproof glass at the dehumanizing, rain-blurred landscape. My fresh dressings already felt sticky with blood.

The cops had picked me up outside the Intercontinental Hotel, soaked in blood. Some of it was mine, most of it was someone else's.

I spent the next six weeks handcuffed to a hospital

bed, recuperating from gunshot wounds. By the time they shunted me into the system my left hand had turned the color of ham-fat, and my bruised skull was rattling with blood-streaked nightmares.

I didn't talk. I couldn't have, even if I had wanted to. My mouth had been shattered, and I was drinking my meals through a straw…

A drawling voice interrupts my reminiscence. "I get it. The only innocent man in Channings Wood. You and the rest of these motherfuckers. You don't know how tired I get of hearing that shit."

I look up. It's Diggs, the prison governor. We haven't crossed paths yet, but they say that he is a lazy, malicious host. His office is bare, his bookshelf is empty – save for a dog-eared copy of The Art of War.

"In the midst of chaos, there is also opportunity, Mr. Rey."

I shrug. Talking still feels unnatural. I certainly don't want to get in a discussion with this psychotic.

"They say you used to be good at finding people. Am I right, Mr. Rey?"

Past tense. I used to be good at a lot of things – before I got chewed up and spat out by the Paignton meat-grinder.

"Who says?"

The words feel thick and strange on my tongue.

He gestures to the manila folder on his desk. It's thicker than a fucking bible. "People."

He nudges it to one side, dismissively. A black and white mugshot slips out of the folder. It is a man named Gilligan. He's dead now.

"Mr. Rey, as much as it pains me to admit it, there are malevolent forces at work inside this prison. Forces outside of my control."

I glance up at the mirror behind Diggs' desk. My hair has grown out and my beard is thick like a Brillo Pad – wiry and streaked with grey. I've just realized that it is the same color as my prison-issue sweatshirt, but at least it covers the ragged scars around my mouth.

"Organ harvesters operating within my prison, Mr. Rey. Do you know how that makes me feel?"

I shrug. I'm tempted to say to do something to my organ, but I keep my ruined mouth shut.

"Angry. It makes me fucking angry, Mr. Rey."

Out of his office window I can see the churned asphalt of the exercise yard. Next to the yard is a gravel pit. This shit never made the newspapers. That must be where they bury the bodies.

"I want you to find these men for me."

I notice a small scar next to his mouth. It seems to twitch involuntarily.

"Listen, Mr. Diggs. I just want to keep my head down and serve my time... What's in this for me?"

He removes his glasses and wipes them on his official prison service tie.

"I won't lie to you, Mr. Rey... I have the power to make life very unpleasant for you during your stay."

I nod. It will take some doing. My life is already pretty unpleasant.

I stand up abruptly and knock the manila folder off the desk. I crouch down, turning my back on Diggs as I pick it up. I stash a handful of photos down the waistband of my jogging bottoms and place the folder back on his desk.

Diggs glares at me over the top of his glasses as I shuffle out of his office – the small scar next to his mouth still twitching.

"One week, Mr. Rey, or I'll have someone unpick your stitches with a fucking spork."

Part 2: Time Is For The Uninvited

Grice is waiting in the corridor for me, baton already drawn. He's the chief corrections officer, recognizable by his heavy scarring. People say that he is the power behind the throne, and I'm inclined to believe them.

"What did old man Diggs want with you, inmate?"

I shrug.

"Standard welcome talk, I guess."

"You've been here four weeks already."

I shrug again.

"I guess I'm a forgettable kind of guy."

"I've read your file – somehow I doubt that."

He gestures vaguely towards Diggs' door with his baton.

"Just remember who runs this joint. There is truly no sadder sight in life than a control freak who has lost control. "

He laughs grimly.

Rumor has it that Grice organizes the bareknuckle kill-pits and keeps the narcotics flowing. If there is a black market organ trade going on, he must surely have some degree of knowledge about it.

The large scar that bisects his face looks like it was caused with a blunt knife. He grins malevolently, and his face seems to fold in on itself.

When I get back to my cell I clamber up the ladder on to the top bunk. I rub my bloodshot eyeballs with bruised knuckles. The greasy stain on my thin pillow looks like the shadow on a diseased lung.

I flick through the stolen mug shots. Like the photo of Gilligan in Diggs' office, they all have thick black crosses over the faces. In the half-light of my cell they look like diseased ghosts. I match names and aliases to the pictures. Meat-Rack. Herman Strange. The Gunrunner. Maxwell Grinley. The Plastician. Jesus, there is even a photo of my uncle Alvin. I knew all of these men, but I stare uncomprehendingly at their faces.

As soon as the cell door creaks open I stash the pictures in my pillowcase. It's only my cell mate Noodles. He's quiet to the point of being forgettable.

I'm not sure what he is in for – something white collar by the look of him. He nods a greeting and climbs onto his own bunk, clutching a battered-looking library book.

The pictures are clearly visible through the cheap fabric of the pillowcase. I will need to find another hiding place if I want to keep them.

There are some degenerate bastards in this place who steal crime scene photos off their lawyers. They trade them like football stickers in the canteen – passing wank-stained pictures under the table to one another. I'm not handing any of these photographs over. My crimes are my own business.

Part 3: Heavy Generator

In prison, the man with the most jail-time usually runs the show. That technically makes Dirt Dog the top dog in Channings Wood. They say he was arrested after stealing a stash of diazepam from a pharmacy. It wasn't worth much, but he hit a cop with an axe when they tried to arrest him

Dirt Dog doesn't look like anyone's idea of a top dog. He looks withered and skittish.

He leans back and exhales a thick trail of smoke towards the light fitting.

"Shit – no one in this prison stays powerful for long. They are either wondering how to keep hold of it, or wondering how they lost it."

He doesn't so much talk, as he croaks through drug-ruined lungs.

"I mostly keep myself to myself these days," he says. "Social interaction is bad for my health. These ladies are all I need to get by."

His cell is wallpapered with blown-up pornographic magazine covers. Some of them are so large they are bigger than life-size, and I'm finding the full-frontals particularly distracting.

Dirt Dog has a fathomless expression and a guttural laugh. He deploys them like a one-two punch.

"My friend: if it is surgery you want, all roads lead to motherfucking Shaolin."

I nod thanks and leave his cell, taking a shortcut through the recreation room.

There is a bloodstain the shape of Paignton on the pool table, and it makes me feel weirdly homesick. Otherwise, the room looks bare. There are no cues, no balls – all long since repurposed as melee weapons.

I look back towards Dirt Dog's cell. He is standing in the doorway, gazing at me through burned-out pupils.

Part 4: Morphine Chicks

S-block is known as Shaolin, on account of the heavy Chinese inmate contingent. Triad money flows within these walls, and opium papers over the cracks.

Sweet-smelling dope-smog clings to the low cellblock ceiling. The smoke is so thick I can barely make out any of the haunted-looking faces peering out of the open cells.

Beautiful Chinese girls in tight, low-cut silk dresses lean against the walls. Beauty makes me nervous – it always has – I scratch my beard and look away. They are not girls, of course. Even in a prison this lax it is tough to smuggle a real girl in. In Channings Wood, penitentiary pussy is where it's at.

The Cantonese crew have their own surgeon. He's a drunk – struck off for malpractice – and performs favors in exchange for prison hooch. The hooch is rancid, bile-colored filth. It's made from apples, oranges, ketchup, sugar and stale bread, and fermented in a sock or a Ziploc bag. I've tasted it a few times. It tastes like shit, but it is effective, especially on particularly dark nights, when the sound of blood-slick blades plunging into tight flesh won't leave you alone. When the grunted sweet nothings of shit-streaked sex sessions reverberate off the greasy brickwork and into your skull, nothing else hits the spot.

I had heard that the surgeon was fond of cutting guys open and giving them fake breasts made of scavenged medical waste, but these girls are a cut above. Who knows? Maybe there is a new doctor in the house.

A man with a badly rewired jaw catches me looking at the girls. He speaks out of the corner of his mouth, "Mother nature can be a merciless cunt, right Rey?"

I flinch, but Rollie Fingers only offers me his hand.

He runs S-block. His real name is Roland Fong, and he is one of the few Cantonese inmates that I know well. His father died when he was six and got adopted by a local mobster called Malcolm Chung. When he was old enough he started to manage one of Malcolm's stroke 'n' poke joints. The job didn't pay well, and he ended up inside after getting caught driving a truck full of uncontrolled substances across the Tamar Bridge. In another lifetime I used to do jobs for Malcolm, too. I found the experience similarly poorly paid and equally deflating.

"Welcome to Shaolin, my friend. How do you like this little set-up?"

"Nice. Not dissimilar to that rub 'n' tug joint you used to work in…"

"It was a stroke 'n' poke joint – small but crucial

difference, my friend. And I didn't work there – I managed the fucking place."

We both laugh. I haven't laughed for a long time. It feels strange, but not unpleasant.

"Listen – I'm looking for the inside track on an organ harvesting ring – operating inside the big house."

He gazes at me curiously.

"I've heard rumors. Chinese whispers, if you like. Dark shit, man. Not my bag. I'm all about the pleasure nowadays. There is a new crew doing business across the yard. They call themselves the Gravediggaz. They are small in number, but they don't fuck around."

"How can I find them?"

"Try asking for a kid named Lamont. Goes by the name Golden Arms. On the outside he used to run with the Hillside Scramblers – you remember them?"

I shake my head.

"Me neither. Anyway, he should be able to hook you up."

We bump fists.

"Stay safe, brother."

Part 5: Get Your Meat Lumped

"I'm looking for Golden Arms."

I don't direct the question at anyone in particular. I just spit it at a crowd of thick-necked men who are standing smoking in the exercise yard.

The sky is gunmetal grey, and the air feels positively murderous.

"No you're not, son."

The big man's name is Tug Daniels, but everyone calls him Iron Lung.

His eyes are blank and bloodshot. He hits me like I'm a heavy bag. I suspect he's showing off.

Someone starts to chuckle, but the laughter dries up as quickly as it starts.

I look up, into the semi-circle of angry faces.

Then they start to stomp me with their thick-soled prison shoes.

I wake up in the prison kitchen, slumped against a chest freezer. It could be hours later, it could be days. My jaw aches, and my grey sweatshirt is splattered with blood. Nothing seems to be broken, bar maybe a rib or two. At least no one fucking cut me.

The Chef is sitting on a stool in front of me. He leans forward on his elbows, cigarette hanging lazily from his mouth, thick Cuban link chain dangling from his neck. When he sucks on the coffin nail his skin goes transparent, and the bones in his face protrude like a skeleton.

He passes me a bag of frozen peas. I press it to my busted jaw, gratefully.

"Thanks, Chef."

He smiles indulgently, and lays a thick hand on my shoulder.

"Does it hurt?"

"Only when I breathe."

He shakes his head with a sad smile.

"Man, you get up in people's faces, start asking

questions like that, these knuckleheads are gonna put the hurt on you. Golden Arms went missing last night. Dragged out of his cell after final count. His friends are a little, uh, sensitive about the situation."

"Thanks for the heads-up, Chef."

He passes me a napkin. I assume it is to mop up some blood-loss or other, but when I open it up I realize that he has written a time and a place on the cheap paper in marker pen.

By the time I look up he has vanished.

Part 6: Death Whips Rolled Up

I have a knack for self-preservation, but every close shave leaves a scar. The parts of myself that I have left behind sometimes feel more interesting than the parts that remain – like a wild animal that has chewed through its own leg to escape a trap, and left behind a paw.

These are the thoughts that occupy me as I descend into the bowels of Channings Wood.

Inevitably, there is a C.O. guarding the stairwell to the basement. He is a scrawny, unimposing man, who seems to be drinking his dinner. Upon closer inspection, I realize that he is an ex-cop named Tony Starks.

"I didn't realize you worked here, Starks."

"I don't work very hard, if that makes a difference..."

I pretend to laugh, as I step forward and jam the half-bottle into his mouth. His head crunches into the exposed brickwork, and he hits the deck.

I retrieve the bottle from Starks' mouth, and wipe

the bloodied glass lip on my sweatshirt. I take a deep glug.

It sure beats the prison hooch I've been fucking with recently.

I walk down the stained grey concrete steps into the hissing gloom. I think I can hear pigs squealing, until I remember that I'm in a prison…

Part 7: Wet Tissue

Sweat oozes down my forehead, blurring my vision. My guts feel like they are on fire.

The basement has a harsh, sinister smell – like nothing I have ever experienced before.

As my eyes adjust to the dank light, the first thing I see is an inmate is hanging from a ceiling pipe. He looks like he has been quartered.

The hole where the kid's stomach used to be is a mess of purple and yellow fat. I stare at it with a mixture of nausea and fascination.

It isn't the worst corpse I have ever seen – last year I saw an already-fat body bloated to twice its size with sea water – but it is probably the worst one I have seen since I have been inside.

The deeper into the basement I get, the thicker and wetter the rancid air feels. Bubbling black liquid seems to trickle towards the gutters. The room feels hot with bodies, but all I see is a smashed heap of human bones in the corner.

Grice emerges from the gloom, a ruined butcher's smock covering his pristine C.O.'s uniform. He is holding a scalpel in one hand, his well-worn baton in the other.

"You."

I nod.

He comes at me with the baton, and I smash Starks' vodka bottle on the greasy brick work behind me. Grice swings at me like I'm a fucking piñata, and the bone-crack almost makes me vomit. As he is preparing for another shot I thrust the jagged glass into his stomach and twist. He tries to scramble away from me, but the buckled concrete floor is sweaty with guts and other viscera, and he loses his footing – plunging headlong into the bone-colored human wreckage.

"How many kids have you sliced up, Grice?"

He stares at me with dull grey eyes, and coughs up a mouthful of blood.

"Enough."

My left arm feels like it has been shattered, so I retrieve the baton with my right.

"Why do you even fucking care, Mr. Rey?"

I weigh up the question. Then I weigh up the baton in my right hand instead.

There is a nasty crunch and blood spurts from his mangled nose.

"No reason."

I pocket the scalpel and start to drag Grice across the basement and up the stairs by his hair, leaving the odor of decaying flesh behind me.

It's time to see Diggs.

It's time to get paid.

11

Laura Lee Bahr

THE ONE WHO SWALLOWS THE SEA
(I CAN'T GO TO SLEEP)

I am awake, drowning in nightmares.

The Men in Suits are busy tonight, crawling all over this town.

Flies spying with 6,000 little eyes, the Men in Suits see the scariest shit as candy. They lay maggots as they move, boring down into the flesh of every living thought, consuming our minds from the inside out.

I lie staring at nothing, trying to get the screens behind my eyelids to stop projecting the rapid-fire movies of the horror of how hopeless it all seems. You struggle and push and push and struggle and with a blip they have you bleeding out and no one cares about you any more than they do for the animal between a bun.

All I am to them is meat.

But it doesn't matter what I am to them. Tomorrow is my battle. Futile or not, I will fight.

But I can't go to sleep. I can't go to sleep. I can't.

I am so scared. So scared that I call out into the darkness of this room:

"Help," I say. "Help. I see Jackie Kennedy, holding her husband's brain. I hear his brain, spilling out in screams of *no no no no I wasn't ready to go!* I feel the fires that burn millions into ash, I ache in my limbs for the discarded, dismembered, destroyed...but still I must face down my own death. Help me, Jesus. Help me to sleep so that I may awake and fight well for a better day."

A miracle happens, then. Jesus appears.

His eyes are obscured in a shroud, but His heart is beating, bleeding, glowing. It is outside his chest floating in a fire, like it does in all those paintings where He points at His heart like "look at this freaking heart, will ya?"

And if that wasn't miracle enough, He speaks. "I am here," He says, and His voice is a ringer for Isaac Hayes. "I am here for you."

"Wow!" I say, of course, amazed. "Thank you so much for coming! I am very honored you actually came."

"The one set of footprints is where I carried you, just in case you were wondering," He says.

I wasn't, but I thank him anyway for letting me know. "So, here's the thing," I say to Jesus. "I have to sleep, but I can't go to sleep. Can you help? And not just with the sleep, but if you could help me win this big fight I have tomorrow, well, that would be really righteous."

"The fight is important," He says, "but you cannot win if you lack courage in your heart. You must be brave."

"Right," I say, "But that's the problem. How can I just 'be brave'?" All of my fear floods back in. "Can't you see how frightened I am? How messed up everything is in the world, and in just my piece of it? Don't you know that I heard that scream of a woman down the street, and I did nothing but lie here in the dark and hope I wasn't next? Don't you know that I cannot ever walk at night for fear? But sometimes, also, I am too afraid even in the day? Don't you know that I try to hide my face, my body and stare no one in the eye knowing that at any moment I could have to fight for my very life — just because I am meat to them? Don't you know how I quiver, not just from the fear of the Men in Suits, but of *all* men? How can I be brave knowing what it is that they do? What they did, even to *you*?"

"Shhhh," he says, his voice in that Isaac Hayes sigh, and I can almost forget for a moment and go under, his heart a night-light ... but no, it is too disturbing if I look too closely — and then I am wide-awake again thinking about how His heart is bleeding as it beats, bleeding, beating, bleeding still.

"I will tell you a story so you can sleep," He speak-sings, and I can stop staring at His heart and lose myself again in his voice. "Do you know the story of the Six Sisters of Shaolin?"

"Um..." I say, thinking of some stories that sound similar that I sort of know, but He has already started:

"In the quiet mountains of Shaolin, six sisters lived happily, caring for each other and the monks at the nearby monastery. Each sister looked exactly alike, and though the sisters would rotate who brought the monks their meals, the monks believed that it was the same woman. The sisters looked identical, but each had a unique special power. One sister could see anything at any distance, even through space and time. The second sister could hear any sound, even the heartbeat of the earth at its' core. The third had unbreakable bones, the fourth could never be burned, the fifth could sing to make anyone move, even the mountains, to whatever rhythm she sang, and the sixth could swallow the sea for seven minutes."

I don't want to interrupt Jesus' story. I appreciate that He is here and all, and trying to tell me a bedtime story, but I really would prefer an answer to my question. So, I just remind Him:

"But how does this story answer how I can be brave, knowing how pervasive my enemies are? Knowing how they torture and kill — even you, no offense... but they tortured and killed *you*!"

"Shhhhh...." He says gently, and it is like a beautiful breeze of a sound that quiets the storms in my mind, and I can listen again as He continues in that sing-speak voice: "Each morning, the sixth sister would walk down the mountain, past the small village and to the edge of the sea. Secretly, she would swallow it, and collect the shining fish for her and her sisters and the monks of the nearby monastery to eat.

"Now, one morning as the sixth sister returned from the edge of the sea, three fishermen saw her with her basket of fish. 'How is it that she has caught so many fish this morning? We were up very early and caught nothing,' said one. 'Every morning no matter how the fish are jumping she brings home a basket just the same,' said the second. 'We must find out her secret,' said the third.

"The next morning, they followed the sixth sister

to the edge of the sea, and watched in amazement as she swallowed it, and then simply picked her fish up off the ground. Well! They weren't going to just watch, because now for the taking, was not just plentiful fish but sunken treasures, beautiful corals and rare shells. And they ran out to collect what they could.

"The sixth sister was dismayed that her secret had been revealed, but far more concerned that the fisherman seemed to not understand that they had a limited time.

"She could not hold the sea for longer than seven minutes, and she waved and waved for them to come back. Oh, they saw her waving, and the men made fun of her, mocking her as she waved at them, and then they ran further out and away. And try as she might to get them back, she could not. And at last she could not hold the great waters any longer.

"And the sea burst forth from her mouth, and the men disappeared beneath it."

"Oh, right! I know this story," I say. "The villagers put her on trial for the drowning of the men and try to execute her: first by hanging or beheading, and the sister whose bones can't be broken takes her place. Then they try by burning, and the sister who can't be burned takes her place, etc. etc. and each sister's special power saves her and she tag teams the next one. But really it goes a different way than what you're saying."

"Okay, you tell it, then," Jesus says. "You know it so well, you tell it."

I hadn't meant to be rude, but I do think He should know how it really goes, so I say, "So the first sister — who can see anything, even through time and space

— looks out and sees the villagers coming. She sees what is going to happen to her sixth sister, that she will be tried and condemned to death. But in looking at the injustice of this act, she starts to see all the injustices that have ever happened and will happen, and she sees all the evil that was ever in the hearts of human-kind, and all that she sees is too much horror and her eyes burn and burn with tears. And she goes blind.

"And the second one — who can hear anything at any distance, even the heart-beat of the earth — hears first the cry of her sister, who is now blind, and that cry begins to echo into the cries of mothers and fathers, daughters and sons, friends and lovers for all that is lost now, all that will be lost forever, and all the people of the world wailing to God for their broken hearts. She can hear the rumblings of the earth as it moves, and she can hear the screams of the suffering of humans until it dims every other sound. And she becomes deaf.

"And then with their misguided cries for justice, the villagers grab the third sister to be hung, they hang her from a huge willow tree, but she does not die. No, for she is the one with unbreakable bones — and her neck cannot be broken — but she just hangs there, year after year after year, swinging in the breeze, for they never let her down — her eyes always seeing those who come to taunt her, to eat picnics beneath her hanging body, who yell insults up at her.

"And the villagers steal the fourth sister and put her to a stake to be burned. Even though she is the sister who cannot be burned, they don't care. So her skin never melts and she never becomes ash, but they just like looking at her face through the curtain of flames, and they just keep the fire going. And she is there, in the fire, still, not burning. And they joke, and roast marshmallows and name the names of all the martyrs and witches they have burned and ask her through the roar of the fire if she can see them in there, too.

"And the fifth sister — who can sing any song to make anyone move — she goes to the monastery, and she sings a song to the peaceful monks that makes them grab weapons of war, and move to kill the villagers who have tormented her sisters. The songs of war become the only songs she sings, to make people march and march on to slay each other. War, war, war, forever, for vengeance for the horrors her sister saw that made her blind, war for the sounds of terror that made her sister deaf, war for her sister who hangs forever, for her sister who burns eternally, and —"

"What of the one who swallowed the sea?" Jesus interrupts, "in your story, what of her?"

"Oh — see you told it wrong at the beginning," I say, forgetting who I am talking to, and that perhaps I shouldn't correct Him. "That poor sister, who swallowed the sea, she has it worst of all. Because it wasn't three fisherman who followed her, actually, but a school of children. They were all very hungry, and they all promised to follow directions exactly, and she thought she would make sure they all got plenty of fish to eat, but instead, they were all distracted and forgot to listen and started playing.

"They didn't see that she was jumping up and down, telling them all to come back. They didn't know that she held the water in for longer than she possibly could. And then her cheeks finally just burst, and the sea came out in a huge wave that drowned all the children. No one can ever forgive her, not herself, nor anyone else. She can never be forgiven. Her mouth is broken now and can hold nothing now, so she just looks out, onto the sea, looking for the faces of any of the children, hoping one is somehow still alive, and can swim back to shore."

It is quiet in my room but for the beat of Jesus' heart, and mine too.

"That is a very sad story," Jesus says. "Not the way I was going to tell it, but I must admit it has a certain ring to it. Do you think telling the story that way can make you brave in your heart for your fight tomorrow?"

Well, shit.

"No," I say. "Not at all. It makes me feel the same way I was feeling when I called for you in the first place to help me sleep and didn't listen, but I guess that's the problem. My thoughts are so loud I can't hear anything else, not even your voice, even though it has a divine message and sounds like Isaac Hayes — but if the voice of God cannot quell my fears then —"

I hear a rumble, a roar like water, like thunder, like the earth itself shaking on its' foundations. A tornado of sound takes out everything I thought, felt, did, think, feel, do, will think, will feel, will do, to become just this sound and this sound alone.

And now I know what I truly fear, not the Men in Suits, not the men of the world, after all, but God, creator and destroyer. This roar that promises not just me, but all of us, can be swallowed back into itself and we will all just disappear as less than a thought in the universe's expanding mind. This sound is all there is.

But then it becomes still. And I can see the glowing heart of Jesus again. That was just the sound of Him clearing His throat.

"You have told your story," He says, "now hear the ending of mine: The Six Sisters of Shaolin always survive. No matter what they see. No matter what they hear. No matter how many innocents are swallowed by the sea in ignorance. They always survive because one always gives her special power to save the life of the other. Alone, no sister could survive, but, together, each giving her unique gift to redeem the other, they all live happily and simply for the rest of their days."

"Oh," I say. "I think I understand." Even though I don't. I sure don't want to hear that rumble voice again.

"Sleep now," He says.

"But Jesus," I ask, very, very quietly and nicely, "In this story, which one am I? Which is the one that is a metaphor for me? Which one of the Six Shaolin Sisters am I?"

But He isn't answering in a voice anymore. He is answering in symbols, writing each of the words that I am on the backs of my eyelids. And my eyes follow me in each of the letters back and forth until they become just a character in Chinese, the one for the sea.

And this word becomes not flesh but water, water pouring out of a mouth that could hold it no longer and the waves as it gushes forth are my lullaby. And the water rocks me, and all of us (the horror, the meat, the unforgivable) away.

Empty, I float gently, and need nothing but a dream.

12

J David Osborne

PCP AND METH AND MOLLY AND ALCOHOL, AND NO SLEEP

Chris Barrett took it all and then he cut himself, he watched himself do it, watched the drawer open, that was a drop off a cliff, then he took the knife and that was another fall, that was another time the snake whispered to him, that was another time he fell again, descending.

He held in his left hand the head of a child that talked to him. The right hand unbuckled his belt and pulled down his pants and grabbed the sharp kitchen knife and ran the point up and down his shaft, teasing himself, feeling the lights getting brighter and him forgetting how to say the lights and the space he was in were shrinking.

He opened the sliding glass door and the ocean air wafted over him and his hands were empty and his hands held every knife and he cut into the base of his dick, pulling with the other hand, watching the skin resist and pull and cutting that too.

He felt nothing.

He jumped and tossed his dick off to the side and felt the blood and urine and felt himself falling more and he thought he was on his couch falling into the cushions. The snake curled around him and licked his ear and he fell into the ocean air resting on the blue like someone set it there for him to fall through dickless.

After severing his penis with a kitchen knife and leaping from a second story window, Chris Barrett had a tough time reaching his friends. A few of them visited him in the hospital. Oddly, they were mostly folks from a long time ago, people he felt like he'd met in passing when he was a different person. It made sense to him: he wouldn't want to visit him either. He hadn't had a record deal in quite some time, and he'd become too fond of PCP and meth and molly and alcohol, and no sleep. Still, he was bummed that, even though the doctors were able to reattach his dong, sliding a tube down the urethra and out the other end, into the urethra poking out of the red bloody stump like a dried up volcano and sewing it up, his junk would never work right again. And that most of his circle didn't really seem to care.

Cutting off your dick and jumping out of a window and surviving, you'd think, would be the closest thing to going to your own funeral you could get. You'd think everyone who cared would come to see you, to try and suss out what exactly went wrong with this person who seemed so well put-together. But nobody thought

Chris was well put-together. So he guessed it made sense.

One of his visitors showed particular enthusiasm for Chris's condition: his manager, Bob. Bob burst into the hospital room, red-faced and sweaty from the hike up the stairs, or maybe just from being excited. Bob weighed about three hundred pounds. "This is our ticket!" Bob said.

Chris looked up from his phone. "Hey, Bob."

"Hi. Look, think about this. Think about all the people who cut their dicks off. They're all rich now!"

"Like who?"

Bob thought about it. "That guy who did porno."

"He sounds cool."

"Anyway, I've been reading this book. This guy says that the best thing to do when adversity strikes is to turn it into an opportunity. So, what is the adversity we're dealing with?"

Chris thought about it. "That I cut my dick off."

"That's right! So how do we turn this into an opportunity?"

"I don't know."

Bob fussed with his satchel for a moment, then brought out a stuffed animal. It was shaped like a dick, with eyes and a mouth and two angel wings attached. "Meet Dickwing, the dick with wings."

"Did you sew that yourself?"

"What? No. Look! It's Dickwing!"

Chris frowned. "Honestly man, I'm just kind of bummed that none of my friends are showing up."

Bob waved his hand. "Forget about them." He shoved the plushie in Chris's face. "This is the future.

Don't worry about the past. You know I've always been there for you. This is how we turn lemons into lemonade."

Chris held the stuffed toy in his lap. The googly eyes looked up at him. Friendly.

He sighed. "Whatever, man. Do what you gotta do."

The truth was Chris couldn't believe what he had done. Memory occupies a strange space. He could go back and inhabit the time he sat on the couch watching television with his mother, he could inhabit the time he bought soda from the gas station, but he couldn't go back to the time when he cut his penis off and jumped off a third-story balcony. He couldn't put himself back into his body, and he couldn't remember the snake licking his ear or the fall, the falls, the many, many falls.

He felt the same sense about his present reality. He felt like he couldn't remember it even though he was experiencing it. Everything felt distant and too sharp, too present, at the same time. The media whirlwind was exhilarating.

Bob was right. Dickwings was a pop culture phenomenon.

The story of Chris's wild night had gone viral. All the major news outlets picked it up: Complex, 2 Dope Boyz, Okayplayer, they all had articles and thinkpieces about what this former rapper cutting off his dick and jumping out of a window really *meant* for hip hop in 2016. Bob set Chris's twitter to auto-tweet pictures of

Dickwings at regular intervals. Soon fashionable young people were spotted wearing Dickwings t-shirts, sporting Dickwings hats, and taking lingerie selfies on beds covered in Dickwings plushies.

Chris made the podcast rounds. They asked him about his life, about his kids, about how maybe Sandra texting him that night that he couldn't see them anymore had somehow contributed to his decision to do what he did. But he couldn't give a real reason. He couldn't take the other world back with him. He couldn't explain how, when the fractal patterns became so clear and his crotch glowed like a halogen lamp and everything became so clear, that what he did seemed like the most natural thing in the world. He gave mostly non-answers. Soon, he released a mixtape about his ordeal, titled *Still Mostly Here*. It was met mostly with a yawn. The twenty-four-hour news cycle had turned over, most people already tired of hearing about this washed-up dude with a weird reattached penis. Twitter roasted him. Complex hated the mixtape. Even Pitchfork reviewed it, giving his last artistic effort a 3.2.

One night, Chris had a little too much to drink and passed out on his couch. A booming sound woke him up. He started awake, knocking the bottle of Henny out of his lap and onto the carpet. He cursed and picked up the bottle and set it on his coffee table. He walked into his kitchen to get some paper towels. When he turned on the light, the creature before him made his heart jump into his throat.

Standing in his kitchen was a giant dick and balls. It had two muscular arms, one of which held a sword. Beautiful, feathery angel wings unfurled, knocking salt shakers and pots and pans off his stove.

"What the fuck are you doing in my kitchen?" Chris said.

"Behold," the creature said, "It is I, Dickwings."

Chris wiped the sleep out of his eyes and shook his head. Surely he was dreaming.

"You are not dreaming. I have come to visit you from the Next World."

Any other person might have run away, or checked themselves into a mental hospital. But Chris had done enough PCP and meth and molly and alcohol and no sleep that he decided to roll with it. "Okay. What are you doing here?"

The giant phallus took a deep breath. It spoke through its pisshole. "I come from a dimension much like your own. Whether the Dickwings phenomenon created my world, or the popularity of it signifies the proximity between our realms. Regardless, I have come with a message."

Chris pointed at the thing's balls. "You've got some hairy nuts," he said.

"Those are not my nuts. They are my feet," the creature said.

"Oh, right on."

"I have come to tell you that it is time for you to take your place as a normal, penis-having man."

"My junk looks super weird, though," Chris said.

"I'm not sure."

"You must get a blowjob, Chris," the creature said.

"I don't think…"

"Do not argue with the will of Dickwings!" the creature boomed.

Chris was going to protest but the snake was there, the snake that always whispered and it curled around him and filled his heart and then it struck out its jaw unhinged and the talking dick screamed but it was too late, the snake swallowed him whole, and then he blinked and he lay there plastered to the kitchen floor, unsure of whether or not the tile was made out of linoleum but certain for the first time that he would do what the dead dick said.

Bob had left him. He'd been smart about it, and when Dickwings was hot, he'd ridden that fame to several up-and-coming rappers, and they'd hired him on as a freelance promoter. Any man who could turn a guy chopping off his meat and jumping off a two-story balcony could surely spin their story into something that got people talking.

Chris began hurting again, and taking PCP and meth and molly and alcohol, and no sleep.

One night he was wandering the streets, noting how the steam roiling up from the sewer grate looked like snakes eating each other, when he bumped into a street prostitute named Mandy. She told him her prices and he agreed, and took her back to his place.

They lay on his bed and he told her everything

about himself. "When my kids were born," he said, sighing up at the ceiling, "That was probably the happiest I'd ever been. I don't know why I do so much, though. I don't know why I can't just sit back and enjoy the things that I have. I don't know why all of my friends have left me, and I don't know why she won't let me see my children, and I don't know why people loved Dickwings so much. It was just a talking dick. That shit is retarded. But I also don't know why they abandoned Dickwings so fast. No one is loyal. I miss my daughter. She used to always have this toy gun. And my son. Him and his Xbox. I don't know what to do but I have all these powders and I figure that might be the best thing."

She listened dutifully, then pulled down his sweatpants. His dick looked like a science experiment. The balls looked fine, but the penis crooked off to the side, the stitches still visible. She took it in her mouth and started sucking. Chris held onto the bed. The sensation felt like too much and not enough at the same time.

"I want to just be normal," he said. "I want to just go to work and stare off into space and see everything under those bulbs. Did you know that those bulbs are actually flickering, but it's too fast for us to notice? Some people notice."

Her tooth caught one of the stitches. Chris could feel the skin peel slightly.

"Keep going," he said. She did, tasting copper.

"Mostly I realize that I'm a footnote in a larger thing. I just wish that my footnote was less embarrassing. How do you reconcile being the protagonist with being the bit player?"

The snake whispered in his ear. Mandy sucked too hard and he could feel his dick separating at the base.

"Keep going," he said. "Don't stop."

In his dreams Chris Barrett is on the Breakfast Club and Charlamagne and Envy and Angela have all severed their genitals and placed them on the table in front of them and they interview him about his career with straight faces and their pants soaked in blood and urine and he tells them that you have to take a risk sometimes, and that he is proud, and that they have all chosen the correct train and he's falling from the balcony again and the son is carrying his penis on his back and the snake has wrapped its tail around him and begins to lick his ear again, and when he wakes up he takes PCP and meth and molly and alcohol, and he never sleeps again.

13

S.L. Dixon

THE RIGHTEOUS HUNT

Through a grimy, dust-caked window, a yellow cloud hovers inches from the cracked street, moving forever as if driven by malicious intent, hungry for the great grandchildren of the few survivors of the species.

Shoes Lee stared through an ancient black rubber gas mask handed out to every member of his former community, back in the times before a cloud took them all and turned them into sour meat.

It was chance that put him in an old diner. It was sense that kept his mask tight to his face while he hunted.

Diners were good for hope, the emblem flashed often and now and then a message. Toilets were better. Picnic tables all right too. High school locker rooms were the best. His father told the story, passed down from generation to generation and sideways from boy to girl, from boy to boy, from girl to girl, from all to the walls to all the survivors.

Sometimes the walls do talk.

Other hunters surviving the clouds spray painted markers,

Killer bee hive
Wu is here
Long live the chambers!
Forever is tomorrow and yesterday

Those were the good hunters, leaving messages for others seeking the messages.

Bad hunters set out signs and lie in wait,

Three verse inside!

No hunter can turn it down. To be a hunter is to seek, to carry the torch of hope to take things back to the before times.

Shoes sat in a booth and stared around him as the yellow cloud crept into the diner. There was no chance to work, or rest, or eat, he had to sit and wait. His gloved hand pressed tight over the recent fish twine seam holding flaps of flesh together behind his leather pants.

Three rises and falls of the moon ago, back when he had a friend in the cold world, Shoes had come upon a painted W.

"What do you think, Boots?" Shoes looked down to the black and brown mutt wearing canine gas mask over its snout. "Boots, pay attention."

Boots, a mutt with Doberman genes heavy in his pool, looked up to Shoes. The dog was up for anything, but still well behaved and eerily sensible for an animal.

Shoes stepped closer.

"Seems ok, but stay behind me."

The W in fresh red paint next to the door carried the message,

Iron flagged twice

It was enough, a secret message only a hunter knew, one a hunter cannot deny.

Shoes was not new to the hunt nor to the games wrought hunters play. He stepped up the crumbling cement stairs of a three story red brick building, once a specialty school for children with behavior issues. Standing aside of the steel, he pulled the heavy steel door and waited, listening.

Nothing.

Shoes looked over both shoulders, down the avenue in both directions. The air was clear, the sun barely visible, a beautiful day, all things tabulated. He lifted his mask and took a deep breath of the fresh air outside and then one from within the former school.

There was stale smoke from a fire days gone. The floor carried no slip nooses, no bear traps and no trip wires.

"Come on, boy. Stay close."

The man entered and the dog rushed ahead.

Through the first hall, he followed the signs to a set of stairs and he again lifted his mask. The smoky scent was nearer, but no newer.

"What do you think, go downstairs?"

The dog whined in agreement, barking not an option within the mask.

Dim down the stairs, Shoes ran his light over the

vast empty hallways, over the doors, looking for another hint. A red W covered the entire upper-half of a door, the small placard behind the paint reading, *boys' change room.*

Predictable.

The message came to children and teens when their parents didn't listen.

In the times before, the youth caught messages while the adults ignored or pushed aside the impending trouble. Coming before their time, the messages transcribed onto walls and tables, carved, drawn, painted and seen as graffiti were so much more.

Auditory mathematics of the universe.

Those in power and those once aware misplaced the necessary balance and the first yellow clouds appeared.

Mother Earth wanted Her planet back from the undeserving and unaware occupants.

That was then, the people died but the messages remained.

Shoes pushed open the door and lifted his mask for a whiff. There was a new scent, something odd. Chemicals, a pine-scented cleaning agent.

Odd, but not enough to keep him away, he let the dog in and flashed his light around the small-scale room. There was an arrow above the shower area, past the benches and hooks. Boots ran inside and Shoes followed, slowly, training his flashlight on the stony floor. He entered the shower and saw the red paint.

Mask over his face, he did not smell the heavy, close reek of six hunters doused in concentrated floor cleaner. A red arrow pointed to a corner and Shoes stepped forward absent of caution.

Boots, found the stacked bodies behind a shower curtain and investigated. The dog did not have the understanding or the voice to convey what he saw.

The light fell onto the old message, carved in a circle around the familiar ovular W,

Livin' the life of a modern day Flintstone

Shoes' heart thumped in his chest. It was a truth, a message carried on a way for hundreds of years, awaiting a hunter to collect the messages. Licking his lips behind his mask, Shoes retrieved his notebook from his battered brown leather satchel.

He wrote in pencil,

21. Livin' the life of a modern day Flintstone.

His hands shook with excitement. He shined his light over the room looking for more paint, and then found it. Another W: different artist, but old, likely from the same era.

"Shimmy shimmy ya," he read aloud and transcribed the message into his notebook.

Boots growled.

"Give me your collection," said a gruff and yet high voice, raspy and savage. "Hand it over or this mutt is dead."

Shoes turned to see Boots held by his collar fur and the rubber strap of his mask, a machete held tight to his ear. The figure with the machete was a small woman, small but hardened with time. Bald and scarred, wearing a green gas mask and bulky leathers, made for a woman numerous sizes larger than the current wearer.

"Hand it over or your dog dies!"

"There is no redemption for thieves and

murderers."

"Shut up and hand it over!"

"Ok, ok," said Shoes and held out his notebook.

"On the floor, back over there," the woman nodded in the direction of the shower enclosed by a curtain.

Shoes edged that way after dropping his notebook to the floor, feeling sympathy for this hunter. There was no hope for her. Once she collected enough, it would take her nowhere.

"What has happened to you that you…?"

"Shut up, how many do you have? How many?" she shrieked.

Boots growled and tensed.

"Twenty-two with these two."

"Twenty-two," she whispered, "You are better than the others and this will take me, carry me away from here, forever. I will know heaven! I will know everything and live in the better world! You can watch if you like, watch or die, your choice."

No choice, Shoes dropped down to his knees, and begged for his dog. Life was hard as it was. He did not want to consider his existence without his only friend.

"Ready the floor. I know you have the sacred fixtures."

"Yeah, ok. Let Boots go, please? He is just a dog."

The woman pressed her knife to the dog's throat, "Set up the ceremony and maybe you'll both see tomorrow!"

From his satchel, Shoes took out the chalk, the bag of sand and the eight candles, one for each point of the W. The emblem centered the open stone floor. He lit the candles and put them into place. The sand circled all and

Shoes watched as the woman stepped into the center, grip still tight on Boots, the dog had eased and cooperated.

Her knees held tight against Boots head. With a free hand, she scooped up Shoes' notebook, cleared her throat and read.

Shoes echoed the words, knowing all by heart, even if she stole all she would never take the words unless she ended his life. He heard the latest addition and lowered his eyes as she dropped his notebook and retrieved a slip of paper from her pocket to read from other stolen messages.

He hummed so that the ill-gotten words did not soil his mind.

Three minutes passed before the woman screamed.

"It is all junk, just lore! There is no return! The ruin is forever! This is all a game, a game to lose!"

Boots, jarred by the sound leapt forward. The frantic woman chopped the machete down on the dog's neck; the dog fell, and cried out in pain.

"Boots!" Shoes shouted. His eyes burst into salty showers.

"It's all junk!" the woman charged, swinging the bloodied blade.

Shoes stumbled back through the curtain, falling onto the decaying pile of dead former hunters. He felt a dead man's knife slice into his thigh. The pain burned him past the grief. His hand jammed into his pack and he brought forth his revolver. Ammunition had become unreliable, dampened and dried dozens of times within the seemingly limitless boxes on former shop shelves.

Shoes squeezed four times before he found an active round. The round jumped and slapped a tiny, wet hole through the woman's forehead.

Shoes rolled from the pile of carnage and crawled to Boots, the dog lay panting. Shoes pulled away the mask. The dog bled out in the arms of his only friend. Shoes held on through the night and come morning, he buried the dog and the murdered hunters in graves under the small patch of grass near the entrance.

He left the woman on the steps leading up, a lesson to other evil souls looking to darken heaven and putrefy *forever*.

For two days and two nights, Shoes lie in the long grass next to his only friend in the world. Bodily need forced him to go on. Shoes strolled along the streets unfamiliar to him looking for dried food, onion powder or ground oats, something not sullied by animal or mold.

It was then that he stepped into the diner, a place called *One Step*.

Sitting in the diner, as the cloud rolled by, streamed to his waiting spot, Shoes wondered if it was worth it all without Boots by his side. He considered the final sentiment of the frantic murderer. Others questioned his path, questioned his hope and effort, questioned his religion and the *Chambers*. Many laughed at the hunters, the packs living in their hapless communities, doing nothing to bring about better days, just existing, procreating, gathering junk, ignoring the knowledge and dying ignorant of the universe around them.

"Maybe they are right, what do you think, boy?"

Shoes asked to the empty diner. "Oh right, you're gone and I'm alone."

Shoes lifted his hand from his leg and rose, an idea blooming in his mind. It was all a mistake, the writing in his notebook, words scrolled on tables, symbols painted on walls. There was no return and no hope for the world. It was all graffiti.

He rose from his seat.

"Who do you think you are?" he asked himself, standing at the diner door. "What is tomorrow and the day after, alone, looking for a myth, words taken out of context? What is it all? Just stuff jotted by kids, no path no…" he paused and took a deep breath.

A thought, a sad whim.

He put his hands on his mask. One breath without the filter was enough to sicken him, two breaths was enough to send him sprawling for days and three, four, five, six, a dozen, somewhere amid those breaths, spelled his end.

"No *Chambers* without you, boy."

Tears dripped down onto the interior of the mask as he rested his head against the door as he attempted to work the nerve to complete the act, to find the necessary strength to give up and face the true unknown of death.

Somewhere, deep down, in his mind, Shoes heard Boots whine, heard him bark, felt the soft rubber of the dog's mask nudge his hand, looking for affection. So real, so close.

"I can't do it without you, Boots!"

A bark filled the diner and Shoes spun, dropped his hands from his mask. There was movement from behind the counter. A thin black curl wagged.

"Boots?" Shoes whispered and limped away from the door.

He stepped to the counter, leaned on a stool and looked over, seeing the soft black curl again. It rushed away, into the kitchen.

Shoes raced after the tail that had to belong to Boots and yet couldn't. Boots was gone, dead, forever. And yet, what is forever but a promise from the past?

The black curl turned a corner and Shoes limped faster, his heart banging on his ribs. He came to a closed door, the only option. Dogs can't open freezer doors, especially not dead dogs.

Shoes pulled open the door and called into the darkness, "Boots?"

A bark filled the small space and Shoes froze in place, watching a great blue light carve a W out of the darkness.

Beneath it, in the very order collected over the years, the very order written in his notebook, the lines formed,

1. Can it all be so simple?

2. Only one way and that's my way

And on and on, all the way to the lines he inscribed from the school locker room walls and then beyond to the unknown.

23. So high that I can kiss the sky

24. Feel the power of the final shower

And still, it continued, on and on until the fabled finish.

36. Your seeds grow up the same way.

Shoes Lee lifted his mask and read the phrases aloud, knowing only then that the rest would show. The ceremony was unnecessary. Speaking the words had made this so utterly obvious a smile crept to his lips while he read. It was the power of the message left behind; it was always the power behind the words.

Two-thirds through the list, his heart seemed ready to burst, his vision wavered as the yellow cloud followed him into the freezer.

Boots, back in full doggy form, encouraged the man with a nudge.

Shoes read on, faster and faster.

On his thirty-third message, he felt his body vibrating at an unfamiliar frequency.

At the thirty-fifth message, the yellow cloud seeping into the freezer filled his chest.

"Your seeds grow up the same way," he spoke feeling peace in the final words

14

Aaron Besson

HELLRZA

Marvin sat pleased with himself drinking a bottle of Mike's Hard Lemonade.

A lesser soul would probably say that all the grief he received for buying the rights to Lyphenol-IV from Giddings-Omceon only to raise the price 1700% wasn't worth it. Marvin dealt with lesser souls like that daily.

The looks on their faces when they realized how few fucks he gave made it all worthwhile if the money didn't, which was a ludicrous idea because the deal made a lot of money. Marvin thought the fact that Giddings-Omceon was selling one of the most used antidepressants on the market for such a ridiculously low price was idiocy only matched by the inane price he was able to buy the rights for it.

He swished the light-liquor Lemonade around in his mouth as visions of first quarter earnings played in his head. The usual suspects of lefty octogenarian hand-wringers on the board of trustees bitching about "the public opinion impact" of the price increase didn't surprise him at all. It only made him wish there really were FEMA death camps for the elderly.

He took another small sip when his phone buzzed.

Sighing in annoyance, Marvin pulled up the security app on his phone and answered "What?" He was answered with a static growl on the other end. He thought for what he paid for the place they'd be able to upgrade the communication system to the current century.

"Who the fuck is it?" he yelled.

The growl on the other end became words. "Delivery for Mr. Marvin Scorelli," drawled the voice on the other end.

"Fine. Come on up." Marvin pushed the entry button on the app and ended the call.

Marvin's door buzzed. He snuck his way to the peephole and peeked through, seeing no one in the hallway outside. Breath released in mixed relief and anger, he opened the door and yelled, "What the fuck!?"

Standing at the door was a figure standing barely over four feet tall in a black hoodie, cargo pants, and black leather gloves holding a thin brown paper-wrapped square package. The man's head was down, the hood hiding his features.

"Delivery for Mr. Marvin Scorelli," the hood rasped, his voice thick and low. Gloved hands held the package up to Martin.

Marvin looked at the package like he was being offered roadkill. The deliveryman just stood there, shoulders heaving as he breathed audibly, his outstretched hands not moving. Marvin slowly reached for the proffered package, and then snatched it quickly.

Marvin turned the package forward and back in his hands, unmarked except for his name and address scrawled on the front. "Who's it from?" he asked.

The short figure shrugged and left down the hallway.

"Hey! Hold on a goddamn minute!" hollered Marvin, but it didn't matter; the delivery-man kept his pace and turned the corner.

Shutting the door behind him without taking his eyes off the package, Marvin walked over to the countertop, grabbed a knife from the block, and sliced the wrapping twine loose. He carefully unwrapped the paper until he was left holding an ornate gold and black album sleeve. In the center of the album was a silhouette of a scythe, shovel, and pickaxe crossing over each other.

He almost dropped it when he realized what it was, this was the one-of-a-kind pressing of the Gravediggaz "Chainz of Black and Gold" album. A guy he met at a cocktail party a few weeks ago who worked in the music industry told him that the Gravediggaz had made only one copy of what was the pinnacle of their career, and that it was going on a private auction if Marvin wanted to take part.

Marvin's buddies in the executive lounge never understood his love of what they condemned as "THAT kind of rap." What did those toolsheds know? For them, Macklemore and (when they were feeling particularly raunchy) Kid Rock were the length and breadth of their rap knowledge. Marvin had tried to defend his musical choices more than once, illustrating how he was against "The Man" while for all intents and purposes being indistinguishable from "The Man".

It all fell on deaf ears.

Gently taking the album out of the sleeve, he had to admire the way the album had been printed to look like pure gold, a disc of sunshine. Lowering the needle onto the album and letting it start, he was startled by the horrible sound that emitted from the speakers. It sounded like a cross between a machine gun, a fracking, and the worst elements of dubstep.

Marvin's temper rose again, but he noticed something on the album sleeve.

He picked up and saw that there was some writing in the lower left hand corner. In a hard-angled script it read, "To be played at 33 rpm."

Weird speed for a full-length, but he wasn't about to give up after all he had spent on the album.

He picked up the needle, dropped the speed on the turntable to 33 rpm, and replaced the needle at the start. It was a completely different listening experience right off the bat, but still completely wrong compared to what had been expected. Instead of dirty beats and lyrical flows, his ears were met with what sounded like rocks being thrown down a deep well and a keening violin reel with too much delay, all of this accompanied by the sound of chains tinkling against each other at random moments. When Marvin thought it couldn't get any worse, he would hear a scream of someone being tortured beyond the threshold of pain.

Marvin was just about to take the needle off the record when he heard a voice behind him like velvet and razors say "Aw hell no, dawg. You gotta leave it on now." Marvin spun around in shock, and almost fainted when he saw what stood before him.

A tall, black figure in stitched leather Avirex jacket and baggy pants loomed in the partial darkness of the condo, thumbs hooked in the pockets. Multiple scars created a lattice-work across the face, making the aviator sunglasses hiding the eyes even more pronounced. What Marvin thought to be tight braids were small black chains hanging down the figure's scalp, terminating in small hooks that tinkled lightly against each other.

Marvin felt dread and vomit rising in equal measure. "Wh-who are you?" He started backing farther away, frantically looking back and forth between the nightmarish creature in front of him and something, anything that could be used as a means of defense. His eyes focused on the knife he used to unwrap the album.

He snatched it up and then held the knife far out in front of him, making plaintive little jabs at the unwanted guest who stood 6 feet away.

The intruder cocked his head for a moment then grinned, showing a rusted wire grill laced across his teeth. "Bitch, if you knew who I was you wouldn't even bother with picking up that knife an' just gone straight to the screamin'."

In the blink of an eye, the intruder was standing an inch away from the knifepoint. Marvin shrieked as dropped the knife, then tried to make himself small against the corner.

"What do you want? You want money? Here!" Marvin pulled his wallet out and flung it at the figure. The wallet slapped dully against the leather jacket, then fell to the ground. The sunglasses looked at the wallet for a long moment, then slowly looked back to Marvin. "Bitch," the intruder growled, "you are seriously startin' to insult me."

A whine started to form in Marvin's throat, then died off. "I don't know what you want! Just take the fucking wallet! Take anything in the condo and go!" For all the tough guy role that Marvin showed the world, this was him in his natural state. He hated the intruder for bringing that part of himself to the forefront, but not enough to crawl beyond it.

In a wave, a low spastic rumble came from the figure's throat. From the shaking of its shoulders, Marvin realized he was being laughed at. The laughter stopped but the intruder still wore a wide, blood-stained smile. "Oh, little lamb, I came here because of the album."

"The album?" repeated Marvin, looking towards the gold disc sitting on the turntable. "Y-you want it? Take it! It's yours! Just get the fuck out!"

"Oh, make no mistake, all of that is goin' to happen," said the intruder, "but you're comin' with. You played the album, I came. That, an' the fact you've haven't shown love to the children, to the needy. That part I'm takin' care of for free, on account of you bein' a vile piece of shit."

Marvin scrabbled for the knife and held it over his head in what he prayed was a threatening manner. His tormentor chuckled darkly and said, "Bitch, please." With the sound of flesh tearing, he yanked two of the chains out of his scalp and threw them at Marvin before he could react. The chains sang through the air, one wrapping itself around Marvin's throat, the other stabbing through the hand holding the knife, causing it to drop as the hand spasmed in pain.

Marvin fell to the ground, trying to free his throat and nurse his ruined hand yet failing miserably at both. The intruder strolled over to Marvin and crouched down next to him as he took off his shades, showing his eyelids sewn shut with thick black wire.

In wild-eyed horror Marvin tried to back away from the creature's rancid breath, but found himself backed into a corner. "You want to own this music bitch? Well guess what? Now, you're going to be part of it!" The no-eyed man walked over to the turntable, and with reverence returned the album to the record sleeve. Before everything went dark, Marvin heard a distant church bell ring...

Marvin was jarred from the timeless oblivion he had been wrapped in. If not for his lack of clothes and his new surroundings, he wouldn't have even known he had been unconscious. In a panic he tried to cover his nakedness as he took in where he was.

He was in a huge golden hallway with only dark, cloudy skies high above as a measure of how deep down he was. There were no handholds on the plain bright yellow walls, and climbing out was impossible.

Breathing shallow to the point of hyperventilation, Marvin looked forward and behind him despite both directions being identical. Clutching his wounded hand he started walked forward with uncertainty, confusion, and terror ruling his footfalls.

He heard a maudlin violin reel floating from an unknown direction, cut occasionally with the sound of chains clinking together. The sound of a reverbed, erratic beat weaved around him. He jumped and spun around every time a shriek pierced the air, seeming to get ever closer.

The chains, beats, and violin had covered a third sound, but it slowly started to emerge: a low scraping noise. It was barely audible but started to get louder quickly. Trying to ascertain the direction of the sound was impossible until the source became visible behind Marvin.

A giant silver needle shaped like a huge spike slowly, but inexorably, dragged along the floor towards Marvin, carving a groove as it went. The needle was thick enough to leave absolutely no room on either side to avoid it. Letting loose with a shriek he ran away from the oncoming needle, urine running down his leg in a warm stream.

Marvin fell down, holding out his hands and tried to bargain with the needle to stop, even as he knew that his screams would soon join the others he heard. High overhead, he heard a familiar voice of velvet and gravel say, "Get used to it, I play this album a lot."

15

Sergio Hernandez

LINX

I'm the eyes that are in back of you.
My daughter sleeps behind this gate. Protected
by wood, metal, sheetrock, blankets, and me. You and I,
we dream for something. How many bricks build a house
and how many destroy it? After this, New York will be
a microcosm. "Daddy" Wait. "Daddy." Back to bed my
sakura blossom. "Okay but…okay."

There is no room for knuckleheads Tony. We keep
our circles small in diameter. We celebrate with powdered
doughnuts. Loaded clips end quarrels. We wear masks or
become ghosts. My mind tries to recreate the past, tries
to bring back her mother through sheer mental will. But
there is no will greater than death.
Lou, we're coming from the deadened hallways of
Babylon, lost soldiers with clouds in our veins, our family,

prisoners outliving prisons in cold blocks of concrete. The rich and their immortality complex. Fuck em. No one lives forever, and we're here to prove it.

You're right Tony. We're no one's bellboys. You know whole cities have been erected on the strength of drug money? Billion dollar companies built on clean dirt. Cream is the crop and it modifies all histories. We're not ruthless, but we have priorities. We have to eat, so if someone takes an unexpected trip off a moving airplane, it may be nothing personal but absolutely necessary. So we speak of…

Passion, trust, longevity. We hold the first, let go of the second and plan exclusively for the third. We are a true democracy riddled with the scriptures of artful war. "Daddy you seem so calm, you act like you are in a dream, I heard loud noises last night. I thought they were coming for you. For us."

Please go back to bed. There's nothing for you here, darkness brings the shadows of evil men. But no one's coming for you as long as I'm here. As long as your uncle Tony and I are here you can sleep sound. "Daddy" "Time is running out Daddy. I can feel it ticking inside me, perhaps a small bomb, an impending fate." I know dear daughter, and it'll all be over soon. We haven't reached our zenith.

"It's raining today, my father and uncle are out in the rain, looking for a man who broke into my uncle's house. Didn't take anything. Didn't have the chance I suppose. He ran off at the first hint of danger. The rain feels so light, and yet I know how heavy it is. My father is changing. Perhaps he's going insane. He wants to save us from this. He wants better for me, at least he thinks it's for me. The truth is he's tired. And he can't just sell drugs the rest of his life. They're always at war within. Him and my uncle. No sunlight. We're drowning in inches of rain."

"Outside my father shadow boxes in the dark. I play my phonograph to silence the city. My father and his family move like wolves in sheep clothing. They show nervousness, as if their heads are always under sharpened guillotines. His punches connect with some symbolic opponent. Money is poisonous. I've seen it enter so many veins. Only swords can end the kind of misery that spreads like rivers through the body."

Tony, it is always good to see you. Seeing is one of the few belief systems that is still intact for me Tony. I was thinking of that time we were on the street corner and the foreigner pulled his pistol on you after you slapped him to the ground. Ha-ha. Those were good times Tony. But Lou, those good times each came with heavy prices. That kid shot me through my neck; I don't even know how I'm still alive. Surgery and the kind act of a lost God I suppose. I was just thinking that even though we went through a lot, those times just seemed more simple. I want to go back to those days Tony. We have some very simple times ahead of us Lou, times full of relaxation and dare I say, safety for our families and ourselves.

Daughter do you ever feel like you're in the middle of the ocean surrounded by sharks, and they're all trying to bite you. "I never feel that way daddy" Good. I hope you never have to feel that way. But maybe if you do ever feel that way, you can see it as something positive albeit frustrating. "I'll keep that in mind daddy". Just be original, and you'll be at peace. Your mother is at peace. She was an original, but I will never truly be at peace because it is me that should have exited this earth. "I understand father".

"Uncle would you like some ice water. The humidity today is high. It's hard to breathe." I think it's a mixture of things in the air. The humidity, the smog, the stagnation of the city. I know that you feel something you can't really explain. Know that your father and I are working on something that will alleviate what we all feel. No more fear, or jail, or drugs.
"I remember how beautiful my mother was, how even in death, her blood swirled on the concrete like marbled cake. Even in death my mother remained so sweet. It's easy to blame my father and his clan. But the truth is we were all complicit and it could have been any of us. At the funeral one of my father's friends, his name was Lansky, told me that we must maintain like glaciers of ice. He flashed a diamond necklace and he said, stronger than the ice you see here. My uncle Tony always tells me that I can learn something new from every single person on this planet, especially the people around us, despite them being offensive antagonists at times. Her funeral was also the first time I tried Cristal. They call it the finest wine on earth. I'll stick to water."

There are savages roaming these streets. Sometimes I'm not sure if it's safer on the outside or the inside, though I'm almost positive that prison is a safer place for a lot of us. Police or prison guards, a tough choice. We're trying to evacuate this flawed system, create our own. Plant seeds that will grow healthy. Seeds that will rise up against the beasts that have driven us to perpetual poverty. Our promises to rise up are verbal threats. My mind is shifting in different directions. My daughter feels the tears in the fiber. My brother knows that men have limits and I'm almost there; but the seeds are planted.

"When my father talks about my mother, he often says corny stuff, like her eye's sparkled like glass in the sun. It makes me laugh to hear things like that. I don't laugh too often nowadays. Men have a funny way of expressing their interest in women. At least that's what it seems like to me. I'm sure that the sky is getting lower and lower everyday. I hope my father really does have a plan."

Lou these out of towners make it hard to run business. We're going to have to take care of them gently. Like we always do Tony. Besides, we need to have some material for the bedtime stories we're going to tell our grandkids Tony. Bedtime stories. I like that. Always pack more heat than sunshine on mirrors.

The Ice cream man is coming Tony. What flavor do you like? French-vanilla? Butter-pecan? Chocolate-deluxe? Caramel sundaes? With the cherry on top? Ha. I like them all Lou. You know I do. Just a few more days and we can leave this place. We can celebrate with all the ice cream we can eat. It'll be a time for love. Plus your daughter will be able to live again. The last of the keys will sell this weekend. This is the last time. This is it.

I always wanted a son, until I met you. "Is that why you call me sun?" No. I call you sun because you shine like one. Our dues are almost paid, but given that the last one is death, we're not going to pay that one just yet. Daughter let us not forget that we will always be students of our culture, whatever you define as culture will be something you will learn from. Polish your crown; we're going back to the essence. It's close. It is always good to protect your body from the harsh reality around you, your heart, your ribcage, your chest and solar plexus, guard them because they guard you. I'm tired of howling at the moon like a wolf out of breath.

What do you believe in, heaven or hell? "I believe in both father. I believe that my mother is in heaven, and I believe that we're in hell. It may sound sad, but I think it's good to have something to believe in. If you believe in nothing, then you're not going to have anything to strive for. I strive for things father." Good my daughter. Pack your bags. We're leaving New York. We're going to another coast daughter. Beaches, palm trees, mountains, hopefully some fresher air. No more. I'm giving it all up. Pack your bags daughter. Lets move.

My father tells me that I have the powers to resurrect the dead. As we sit here at the airport watching planes fly by, waiting for our own; I think back and appreciate all the pain. He tells me a good listener is a good learner, and I've been listening to every detail that counts. Listening can drive a person mad. Each gun shot, or let down, or put down. Every physical or psychological slap. But how would I know life without the scars? We're going now to a higher degree. I've never been on an airplane. My father says he's opening a music studio, some retail stores. Says I'm going to run it all after I finish school. My father says cash rules. But I know what he really means is that family rules. He just sees cash as a way to protect us. He tells me that we're just babies, and I agree.

CHRISTOPH PAUL

Christoph Paul is an award-winning humor author. He writes non-fiction, YA, Bizarro, horror, and poetry including: The Passion of the Christoph, Great White House Volume 1 and Volume 2, Slasher Camp for Nerd Dorks, and Horror Film Poems. He is an editor for CLASH Media and CLASH Books and edited the anthologies Walk Hand in Hand Into Extinction: Stories Inspired by True Detective and This Book Ain't Nuttin to Fuck With: A Wu-Tang Tribute Anthology. Under the pen name Mandy De Sandra, he writes Bizarro Erotica that has been covered in VICE, Huffington Post, Jezebel, and AV Club.

He is represented by Veronica Park at Corvisiero Literary Agency.

GRANT WAMACK

Grant Wamack is the author of A Lightbulb's Lament and Junkyard Exotic. He is a weird fiction writer and Navy journalist. You can visit him at grantwamack.com

www.ingramcontent.com/pod-product-compliance
Lightning Source LLC
Chambersburg PA
CBHW032010180726
48283CB00008B/2618